Dear Phil
With Love,
your little sister,
Rita

CROSS OVER

You will fall in love with the Guardi family as you follow them from Naples, Italy to the welcoming shores of Long Island. This tale will captivate your imagination as you travel through a spiritual journey of love, death and redemption. Cross Over is truly an eloquent and inspiring read.

Carol Silva
Anchor
News 12, Long Island, New York

CROSS OVER

An Italian-American Novella

RITA SANTANIELLO MCGUFFEY

WESTBOW
PRESS
A DIVISION OF THOMAS NELSON

This is a work of fiction. All of the characters, names, incidents, organizations, and dialogue in this novel are either the products of the author's imagination or are used fictitiously.

WestBow Press books may be ordered through booksellers or by contacting:

WestBow Press
A Division of Thomas Nelson
1663 Liberty Drive
Bloomington, IN 47403
www.westbowpress.com
1-(866) 928-1240

Because of the dynamic nature of the Internet, any web addresses or links contained in this book may have changed since publication and may no longer be valid. The views expressed in this work are solely those of the author and do not necessarily reflect the views of the publisher, and the publisher hereby disclaims any responsibility for them.

Any people depicted in stock imagery provided by Thinkstock are models, and such images are being used for illustrative purposes only.

Certain stock imagery © Thinkstock.

ISBN: 978-1-4497-3378-0 (sc)
ISBN: 978-1-4497-3379-7 (hc)
ISBN: 978-1-4497-3377-3 (e)

Library of Congress Control Number: 2011962120

Printed in the United States of America

WestBow Press rev. date: 1/10/2012

To my husband Drake,

my first and only love and

to our amazing progeny.

Author's Note

The characters and events in this novella are fictitious but several of the events described are factually historical, especially those concerning the Immigrants' journey to America, the McGuffey Readers and the phenomena of the golden rosary.

INTRODUCTION

It all began at the turn of the century. It was the year 1900 when a young and courageous Michael Guardi left his home in San Giovanni, Naples, Italy to come to America. Within five years, he was joined by his wife Bella and their three children, Alfredo, Giovanni and Chiara. This is the story of three generations of Guardis and the effects that Michael and Bella's uprooting had on their lives. The central character, Americo, more familiarly known as Rico, is portrayed as the victim of what went wrong in his life because of the choices of others, and what went wrong because of his own.

PART I

ASHES TO ASHES

CHAPTER 1

THE SLEEPING PLACE

It was created in the late 1800s as the final resting place for the settlers of a quaint North Shore community on Long Island. The landscape was treed and green, untouched and indifferent to the sleepy hamlet slowly emerging outside its iron gates. The cemetery, pristine and small, was the size of a churchyard, and its charm incidental to its placement in the area. As time went on and the population grew, other more spacious cemeteries came into use and these small "sleeping places" were discontinued. A thriving, upscale residential community mushroomed around our little, idyllic churchyard, making its presence all the more unique. It still served its purpose for the few who were fortunate enough to have held onto their plots bequeathed to them by their ancestors. It is here that our story begins.

The diggers' hands shoveled and turned the soft earth. The results of their labor produced a small mound of dirt and a wee yawning hole waiting to receive the last and youngest of the Guardi sisters to be buried there. It had been ninety years since three of her siblings had preceded Chiara. She had longed to be closer to them in life, and now she would finally be snuggled in next to them forever. Holding their breath for the celestial reunion, you could almost feel the brush of angel wings as they hovered above the hallowed ground.

As the service began at the graveside, Father Giacomo's robes swept over a small disc embedded in the ground close by. The little mound of excavated dirt almost obscured the marker that bore the names of the occupants below. Soon Chiara's name would be added, and their circle of life would be complete. In her mind's eye, Sophia could envision her Aunt Chiara and her sisters playing somewhere.

The time of professional mourners was no longer a tradition in Italian families, and since Chiara was ninety two when she passed, most of her family was gone. Her grievers were few: grand-nephew Giacomo, nephew Carlo, nieces Gina and Sophia and a sprinkling of acquaintances lost in their own thoughts, impatient to get on with life. Nephew Rico was conspicuously absent. He had flat-out refused to attend the graveside services; he said it was because he had wanted Chiara's cremains "scattered in the wind." He had taken the liberty of having his aunt cremated without consulting his cousins, and it was his intention to dispose of her ashes without benefit of a burial. How could he not have known that her last wish was to share this small space with the little sisters who had waited almost a century for her to join them? Two-year-old twins, Guglielmina and Philomena, were the first to sleep in the earthy bunker, and were shortly followed by infant Rosa, barely out of the womb. If their young lives had not been cut short, this story would not have been told.

Staring down at the grave, fleeting scenes from Chiara's life passed in front of Sophia's eyes. She was suddenly aware of a sense of family, which went deeper than memory. What did Aunt Chiara want of them? Gina and Sophia bowed their heads and prayed, "A little light, Lord." Father Giacomo blessed the ground and intoned the final prayer, placing Grandmother Bella's one hundred year old fragile, golden linked rosary on top of the urn before lowering it into the ground. Gina communicated truth through gesture when she poked her elbow into Sophia's ribs, both girls silently wondering, as they glanced at each other, if these were really Chiara's ashes or the remains of some dubious origin. After what had happened in the church that morning, they were afraid their perceptions might be true. They wanted to give cousin Rico the benefit of the doubt, but the shocking events at the church led them to believe otherwise. The family honor, instilled since early childhood, fueled the embers of doubt, and they knew it was their solemn duty to investigate this strange enigma further.

Zia Chiara had confided to her niece Sophia that she had often felt a vital pulling on her spirit; little orbs of light urging her on toward those unlived lives just out of reach. There was that singular moment when the desire to be with her sisters took root in her heart and it grew stronger as she advanced in age. She had come to realize that over the years, she had taken her childhood with her. A sense of deprivation from her youth harbored traces of a poverty syndrome that had long ago dropped anchor in her soul. Chiara simply felt the loss of her sisters' company.

Her parents, Isabella and Michael, were buried at Heaven's Gate Cemetery on the other side of town, and in spite of her great love for them, Chiara had desperately elicited a promise from Sophia to carry out her wishes and be with her sisters for eternity. But for the convictions of Gina and Sophia, such a promise would have been almost impossible to keep.

CHAPTER 2

BY THE BRIDGE

It was May, a month of romance and small tornadoes. These catastrophic elements had lasting effects on two unsuspecting people, who were taken by storm.

They met under the watchful eye of Mount Vesuvius by a stream beneath a bridge in San Giovanni, a coastal suburb east of Naples, one of the oldest and most beautiful cities in the world.

Michael Guardi was on his way home from a wedding, where he had played his mandolin for a newly married couple he barely knew. Because of his reputation as the finest mandolin player in all of Naples, the couple would hire no one else for the celebration. For ten years, Michael had strummed his guitar-like instrument for all those who could pay for his services (and sometimes for those who could not). He had been lining his pockets since he was a boy of sixteen and prayed that it would only be a few more years until he would have enough liras to pay for his voyage to America.

Michael and Isabella had lived in the suburbs of San Giovanni all their lives, but their paths had rarely crossed. The crowds had been too large when they had gone with their families to the Festival of San Gennaro every September. They could have been kneeling next to each other in the Grand Cathedral of Naples and still have been unaware of the other's presence, because it was not yet time for them to meet. In the Lord's perfect timing, they met in the midst of a whirlwind on a bridge connecting their villages, a bridge that would prove to be worth the crossing. With thunder bolt magnitude, divine providence was about to change their lives, blessing them with a love which would span the crossing of an ocean, and after sixty years, when they were no more, giving them new lives which would go on forever.

Because of his long legs, Michael's stride was forced to a snail's pace when he found himself behind the splayed wheels of a hay-wagon being pulled by its equally splayed donkey. From who knew where, out of the clear, sunlit sky, a wicked wind swirled around the donkey cart aiming its whirling darts at the young man's heart. Michael was frightened, thinking the shaky—beamed bridge he was crossing would snap and fall into the river, as it swayed violently, but curiously, its forgiving logs did not give way. The small tornado disappeared as fast as it had come. The only physical aftermath he experienced was the dust in his eyes collected from the loosely tied bales of hay, wildly sliding about on the planks in the cart in front of him. Carried across to the other side of the bridge by the wind, he found himself deposited at the far end, fumbling blindly for the checkered red cloth tied around his neck. Slipping it off, he wiped the gritty residue from his eyes and with gentle swipes, rubbed them until they were red-veined and sore. Looking up, he was puzzled by a sky that was now clear and silent.

Michael was about to continue on his journey when he experienced a phantom lightning bolt that electrified his senses. The intensity of its light was whiter than the sun, casting its illuminating rays on an angelic creature washing her clothes in the stream below. Michael was caught up in this cosmic phenomenon, and he experienced her purity encased in crystal, its facets shooting up shards of light cutting through the windows of his soul, piercing his heart. The clarity of his vision became so intensified that he felt he was seeing for the first time. He was determined to meet this radiant apparition, who, at first glance, had wounded his rapidly beating heart. Shy by nature, Michael appealed to his mandolin, tenderly patting its soundboard. "Dear friend" he said, "I am in need of your dulcet tones to help me win this heavenly creature."

With renewed confidence, his long limbs took a lover's leap from the side of the bridge and landed at her unshod feet. She was not startled at his approach, for she had been observing this tall Adonis of the Bridge as he suffered, with blind indignation, the dust from the hay cart. From time to time, she stopped, mid-scrub, and with a turn of her neck and an upward glance, watched Michael as he cleaned his eyes with the small red cloth, which, with a catch of the wind, looked more like a flag waving for her attention. She was surprised at the deep sympathy she felt when the stirrings in her heart came uninvited. When he suddenly appeared before her, she recognized the cause of her unusual concern.

Holding hands and sitting side by side on the river-bank, they were struck by the magnitude of the miracle blessing them. With intensive urgency, they talked as if the world were coming to an end, and before it did, their lives depended on discovering everything about each other. A pink blush spread over Isabella's cheeks, and her speech had an urgency that came rapidly, quickening his already pulsating heart. Eagerly her words streamed out, not at all strident but with a quiet confidence as she revealed her life.

Her name was Isabella, but in her village, she was called Bella. She could do sums with notches on a stick and lived with her mother on the other side of the river on a small but worthy farm. She could spin the fleece of her sheep to make blankets and warm garments and quilt a bed cover of her own design. A small smile enhanced her dimpled cheeks turning them a deeper red as she told Michael that her feta cheese pie gained compliments at every feast. With natural pride in her people, raising her chin and throwing back her slender shoulders, she proudly stated in a higher decibel that she could make a pizza worthy of her Neapolitan ancestors who had invented it.

Bella stopped to catch her breath. Unlike her usual cheerful disposition, her mood had suddenly changed. "Now," she said, "I must share with you one of life's serious interruptions. When I was a small girl, my father instructed me in the art of cooking, for was he not the head chef at the Grand Hotel in Naples?"

"Until," she said, sighing and lowering her lids, "as sometimes happened in that profession, Papa was the recipient of something fierce, a foul-tempered butcher's wrath. With great accuracy, Mario the dissector aimed his seventeen inch blade at unsuspecting Papa, the effects of which turned out to be fatal. This violent action was the result of an innocent misunderstanding regarding a small cut of veal to be featured on the evening menu. Poor Papa was unaware of the history of the ill-suited newly hired butcher or that the deranged man was subject to raging fits of temper.

The police were called and witnesses provided. Adding to their testimony was the condemning proof of the gruesome crimson splattering on the butcher's apron, making mockery of the poor young calf's unwilling donation for the evening meal. As Papa's life ebbed away from the stabbing, he forgave the man and died in the company of the saints." Bella cupped her hand to Michael's ear, and in hushed tones and with childlike innocence, conveyed to him that Papa was now cooking for the Lord.

It was Michael's turn to please Bella's eager ears with every detail of his existence, but for a moment, he was spellbound by her beauty and unable to speak. Before him was the very likeness of the classically patrician women painted on the frescos by the masters hanging in the Museum in San Giovanni. As he knelt at her feet, he strummed his mandolin softly, its rhythm blending with sounds of the stream that rippled over the small, smooth stones creating a lover's symphony, a harbinger of their life to come. He silently thanked his faithful mandolin, and with embarrassing vulnerability, poured out his heart.

"My passion is art," he whispered, too sacred a calling to convey in a louder voice. He told her of his many visits to the Museo di Capodimonte in Napoli where, in great awe, he studied the frescoed masterpieces of Raphael and El Greco. He revealed his innermost dreams to this exquisite creature, telling her that his ambition was to be a serious artist one day. As all who love know, every detail must be known about the beloved. With the telling, they entered into a deeper state of reality than they would have ever imagined existed, and with holy confirmation, their reflections mirrored their love in the stream below.

Michael and Bella remained by the side of the bridge until the sun fell below the horizon.

Returning to their villages, they noticed that not a person there seemed surprised to hear the good news of their meeting. In appearance, they seemed to belong together, but of more importance, the sage elders prophetically announced that this was truly a mating of the souls.

The following spring, Father Sebastian performed their marriage in ceremonial splendor at the little chapel of San Giovanni de Ponte, a small country church situated between their two villages. As Bella and Michael were taking their vows at the white and gold altar, glorious in its simplicity, exemplifying the Franciscan spirit, a profusion of wild white lilies laced with the breath of the angels enveloped them. The day before, the villagers had set out with large empty market baskets crooked over their arms, eager to reap the magnificent harvest of spring. The chapel was surrounded by fields of wild flowers in full bloom. Soon stiffened backs were evidenced in a few overenthusiastic but well meaning gatherers. Those with more supple spines bestowed their labors of love upon the couple as they proceeded to adorn the entire chapel with the untamed blossoms. The powerful fragrance of wild blue violets was as intoxicating as the introductory catalytic meeting the spring before. The chapel was filled to overflowing with the entire populations of both of their villages, and everyone was dressed in traditional bright colored costumes. Bella was radiant in the delicate white lace tatted gown and veil her mother, Gaetana, had made for her.

The *fiesta* that followed was a time of great celebration. Friends and family from all around the countryside came, some with wine fermented and bottled just for the occasion, many with trays of homemade pasta dishes of every variety. Lorenzo and Beto, baker cousins of Michael's, arrived with mountains of delicate wedding pastries. Young and old twirled and clapped, linking arms, changing direction and circling to form friendship rings; they danced the tarantella, a folk dance that had its origin in their region. The quick steps of the dance and its fast tempo left everyone exhausted, but in light of the occasion, no one seemed to mind at all. In serious games of tag, the children chased each other in and out of the colorful floral streamers hanging from the balconies. After three days, the party was coming to a close. Michael knelt before his new bride and strummed his songs of love with such inspiration that their sweet sounds were carried up to the heights of Mount Vesuvius, and as they descended, the melody echoed in the valley below.

CHAPTER 3

A NEW LIFE

He stood on the ship's deck in the early light of dawn. At sunrise, the first thing Michael saw was the seven brilliant shafts of light pointed heavenward representing the seven continents in the crown of the majestic lady in the harbor. Her torch of freedom made his heart beat faster as the winds of opportunity kissed his cheeks. He had come all the way from Naples to provide a new life for himself and his family. The journey had been arduous, for he had traveled in steerage at the bottom of the steamship with his cousins Lorenzo and Beto, the bakers. When Michael passed through the portals of Ellis Island within the shadows of the Statue of Liberty, he was entering into the gateway to his new world. He was transported by ferry from the steamship to undergo medical and legal inspection at the screening station, which he thought a small price to pay for such a big dream.

The first and second-class immigrants were not required to undergo the inspection that steerage and third-class immigrants had to endure. Standing in the long line for hours, Michael's turn had finally arrived. His name and the answers to twenty-nine questions were contained in the ship's log, which he had filled out at the port of embarkation. Once his legitimacy was established, he was cross-examined during legal inspection. There were only two possible impediments which could cause

Michael from entering the country. One was a contagious disease and the other his likelihood of becoming a public charge. Michael had no problem with either. His health was good, and an American citizen was ready to vouch for his character. Lifting his countenance and making eye contact with the inspector, he surprised himself when his usually soft-spoken voice resounded loudly and announced proudly that a job was awaiting him in Sands Point.

Michael trembled and his eyes filled with tears as his lifetime dream was now within reach. With concerted effort, for he was a man of great discipline, he regained his composure as he awaited the final judgment. Devoid of ceremony and in a very few words, Michael had his answer.

"Michelangelo Guardi, you are granted entry into the United States of America."

The three immigrants from San Giovanni stood on the wharf waiting for transportation to Sands Point, their final destination. The sea air had done its damage to the already frayed rope that was making a brave but unsuccessful attempt to secure Michael's well-worn valise. From time to time, he had to hoist it up on his hip to avoid an embarrassing spillage on the pier. Its contents contained his meager wardrobe, which was molding from its months of captivity in steerage. Patiently he waited for the barge to arrive as he continued precariously to juggle his sack along with his apprentice hod, a tool with a long-handled three-sided box used for carrying bricks or mortar, which was dangling by its strap over his shoulder. This tool and his God-given talents would be the means by which he would accomplish great things in his new world in a way he could never have envisioned.

CHAPTER 4

FIONA

Michael and his cousins were carried by barge from Ellis Island to the snug harbor of Sands Point on Long Island. They went directly to their prearranged room at a run down but comfortable boarding house by the water's edge. It was the last in a row of houses which were few and far between on the broad main street, which was lined with newly planted trees. Shortly after their arrival, they discovered their good fortune, for the owner of their new home lived up to her well deserved reputation. Because she had attended one of the best cooking schools in Milan, her cuisine was the finest on the north shore of the Island. They had good reason to rejoice, for their stomachs would not be subjected to the inevitable culture shock.

To start their day, small cups of espresso greeted them in the *cucina*. Fiona, the owner (as she was called but not within earshot), was from Milan, where espresso was first introduced in Italy and where she learned the art of extracting the nectar of the gods from the coffee bean. She felt it was her mandate as a true Milanese to serve double shots of the thick, syrupy liquid, which never ceased to have an interesting effect on her new boarders. Espresso, was a "quickly, just for you" beverage and took only forty-five seconds each morning for her to prepare. Sipping this steam pressed elixir had an interesting effect on her boarders when it awakened them each day and catapulted them to move as fast as a speeding train. Fiona took it as a compliment when the hair stood up on their hirsute arms and was even more gratified when her boarders stirred their sugar into the caffeinated liquid with their forks. Satisfied, with an epicureans delight, she sliced thick pieces of her homemade bread for the dunking. After her guests broke their fasts in such a grand manner, Fiona could now concentrate on the rest of the meal. Backing off a few paces to observe her own creation, much like an artist at his easel, she viewed her cooking skills as benefiting more savory palates. Waddling about the cucina, wielding her proverbial wooden spoon as a baton, she was ready to orchestrate the job at hand. Out of respect for the contribution of her goat, Almatheia, to her morning feast, she made a wheel of goat's milk cheese that was a work of art. When the wedges were evenly cut, Fiona would wrap them in starched white linen napkins and ceremonially lay them out on the tablecloth, also starched and white, and display them upon the groaning board. (As her clientele grew, she no longer served at table but instead used a long groaning board and allowed her gentlemen to serve themselves.) A pearl-handled knife for paring the fresh-picked fruit, her mother's crystal, and silver vases with wild flowers made the setting look more like a wedding hall than the weather-beaten boarding house by the pier that it was.

After she cleared the breakfast leavings away, and with dramatic flourish, Fiona filled their tin lunch pails with an antipasto of provolone wedges, olives imported from Bella's groves in San Giovanni, prosciutto, seasonal fruit, and delicate iced cakes. Alongside the pails, she placed small bottles of her homemade wine to put a "sparkle in the eye." Their workday started at 5 a.m., and twelve hours later, they returned to be feted with the evening meal. Awaiting her hungry boarders would be steaming bowls of minestrone, meat or fresh fish from the harbor, and gravy made from her garden tomatoes served with homemade pasta. The men worked six days a week and on the Lord's Day attended Mass at St. Peter's at the other end of the wide street, a short walk from the boarding house. When they returned, there was one of her famous chef supreme Sunday meals waiting, and afterward they relaxed behind the boarding house enjoying a few games of bocce on the close-cropped grass, mowed that morning by Almatheia the goat as she filled her belly.

Fiona had been an immigrant herself and knew firsthand the desperation of loneliness. Nothing had distracted her from her pain until she determined to open a boarding house to do what she did best. She cooked for and befriended anyone passing through her small establishment. Within a few years and shortly before Michael's arrival, she had accomplished what she had purposed: she was no longer lonely. Knowing beforehand that the boys from Naples were on their way, she made a special effort to attain more knowledge to help her new boarders feel comfortable in their new home. Fiona walked the half block from the boarding house to the newly established library in the center of Main Street, which was contained in the one-room schoolhouse and consisted of a few books stacked up on the floor in a dusty corner. Whatever she could not find in the meager pile was diligently researched by teacher/librarian Miss Cornelia on her frequent visits to the New York City Library.

Quick to perceive the reasons for Fiona's concerns about helping the new boarders feel more at home, Miss Cornelia found the perfect antidote for her Italian gentlemen's nostalgia: bocce! After fastidious research, she came up with more than a few details on the game. With pursed lips and narrow lavender ribbons flowing from the sidepieces of her small round spectacles pinching the bridge of her nose, she informed Fiona that next to soccer, it was the most popular game in the world and had been invented in Egypt around 5,000 BC, using polished rocks. Pompously pleased with her proclamation, Miss Cornelia continued: Bocce moved to

Greece around 800 BC and eventually found soil in ancient Rome, where beginning with Emperor Augustus, it was considered the sport of royalty. At this point, Cornelia was on a roll and was thrilled to enjoy the ride. Straightening her back and flexing her research muscles, she continued. It was highly recommended by Galileo, that Italian Renaissance man, as a game of athleticism that employed the spirit of competition and rejuvenated the body. Miss Cornelia passionately dug even further into her investigation; her obsessive ways well known to her pupils, who, willing or not, were subject to her overindulgences. (Some of the little listeners were prone to headaches from her excesses, which encouraged them to beg to go home, whereupon they would then tattle on the cause of their migraines, their complaints invariably falling on deaf ears.) Moving away from her desk, Miss Cornelia seated herself on a high stool, which was previously reserved for her less cerebral pupils. Perched up high she resembled a small bird, fluttering her elbowed wings in the telling. She twittered noisily as she explained that George Washington had installed a bocce court at Mount Vernon, and even Queen Elizabeth and Sir Walter Raleigh were avid players. Miss Cornelia alighted from her perch and, adding her last delicious tidbit, proclaimed that in ancient times the Africans played the game with coconuts.

Fiona couldn't wait to impart all of these interesting facts to her new boarders. And then, upon hearing more than they needed to know, Michael and his cousins expressed their gratitude and rushed outside to their makeshift field and even more enthusiastically, if that were possible, played the sport of kings until sundown.

Only after they retired to bed in the dark silence of night did loneliness envelope Michael and his cousins. Finding little solace from their unyielding pillows stuffed with wood chips, they would eventually fall off to sleep, but not before homesickness would feed the longing in their hearts, drenching the chips and by morning leaving the odor of pine on their pillows.

Sands Point was an excellent choice for builders, and Michael had his eye on the future. Walking along the shore before his beloved bocce games one Sunday afternoon, he noticed the large mounds of sand, which went on for miles dotting the shore-line. He pondered the scenic beauty of the north shore and wondered whether grand houses could be constructed of stucco as they were in the old country. As if by instinct, Michael knew that he had found what he had been searching for since his arrival to this magnificent country. The revelation was not only for the houses he would build, but now, at last, he had found the way to create an infinitely more important undertaking. The seed that had been germinating in his heart grew and Michael knew that his only masterpiece would be the one of his love for Bella.

The town was rapidly expanding and bricklayer's helpers were in demand. Within a week of their arrival, with their hods slung over their shoulders, all three were hired on as mason apprentices to skilled bricklayers who had arrived a few years earlier from Michael's home village of San Giovanni. Soon he and his cousins had advanced from carrying the mortar to making and laying bricks, and in no time, he had become as skilled as his teacher was. Within a year, he had been hired on as a builder in a construction crew building wooden houses in and around the up-and-coming community. Michael learned quickly. Once he knew everything he needed to know, he went out on his own and his career took off. As he already possessed the heart and talent of an artisan, he began his new venture by installing outdoor swimming pools for the nouveaux riche on the north shore of the island. He drew on all of his artisan creativity designing mosaic tiled patios to surround the swimming pools he had installed. The rich owners of the mansions considered his work exquisite, and they should know. In fact, his work was said to be equal to the finest mosaics artists in Italy, and, as his reputation grew, he prospered. Within two years, Michael owned his own construction company, but in place of wood, he applied the use of stucco in the building of his old world Tuscan-style houses. His architectural designs became so unique to the area that the wealthy eagerly sought after his services, and soon he was in demand to build their exclusive mansions. As Michael's business expanded, he bought up many acres of land on the north shore of the island.

CHAPTER 5

MICHELANGELO DESIGN AND BUILDING COMPANY

Within four years of arriving in America, Michael was ready to build his own home. The Michelangelo Design and Building Company was doing very well and afforded him the luxury of taking a sabbatical of six months. After employing his three cousins to help him construct his house, Michael selected one of his own choice lots, a stone's throw from the center of Main Street in the charming hamlet of Sands Point. His passion was to build Bella the type of house that would ensure that she would not be lonesome for the old country when she came to live in America. He enlarged on his original Old Tuscan plans to accommodate his new and exciting designs.

The material he used in his building was stucco inside and out. For the exterior, he used multiple coats of sand, and for the cement, he used the new Portland, which he substituted for the customary lime because it was harder and more durable. To have the stucco cling to the interior walls he installed laths of wire mesh and mixed bright pigments to enhance the color.

The trowel was his paint-brush, and with experienced flourishes, he created dense and delicate designs. Michael was ingenious in applying his skill. Using various textures to change the stucco's consistency, he created coarser blends for the ceiling and finer designs for the walls. The most important room in the home would be Bella's very large and bright kitchen. He knew that she would want to spend her days here, using the skills her papa had taught her in her mother's kitchen.

From his redesigned plans, Michael constructed a very high and flat ceiling in the kitchen wing of the house. It was large enough to suit its purpose, his masterpiece of love. He and his cousins then built a scaffold where he could stand while he painted his fresco and use it as a bed where he would fall asleep at night, when light failed, always exhausted from the difficult task. The first time he climbed up to his wooden loft, he was in a light and giddy mood; (probably because of the altitude). Before his first brush stroke, he smiled and his dark curly mustache touched his upper lip. He reminded himself that he had been christened Michelangelo in honor of that other artist who also stood, his body contorted, at heights Michael could hardly imagine and had created his masterpiece on the ceiling of the Sistine Chapel in the Vatican. In the ensuing months, there were times when Michael thought of, and understood how lonely Michelangelo must have been.

His plastering experience served him well in his painting. Timing was critically important; the plaster had to be wet while he painted. If it dried before he completed a section, Michael would have to start over with a new coat. He understood why the masters had said this was the hardest part. The determining factors in how Michael painted his fresco were light, space, and architecture. He was intimately familiar with the actual setting of his picture so that when he painted directly on the vast ceiling with the sunlight streaming through the bay windows, he was at ease recalling San Giovanni, the center of the greatest works of art in the world. Michael knew that Bella's kitchen was the only studio that he would ever need as he painted the place on the bridge where they had first met and fell in love.

He filled a pouch with charcoal dust, pricked it with a needle, patted the pouch over the perforated cartoon drawing he had made of his subject, and transferred it to the wet plaster. The charcoal dust stuck to his hair and as with all serious artists, when they become engrossed in the creative process and do not stop for such things, he solemnly accepted this as his rite of passage.

Plaster had long been Michael's friend, so he was not frightened when he took his first brush stroke on its wet surface. He quickly recognized that it had a life of its own with special needs and appetites for water, paint and the pressures from the brush. It was hard physical labor, but his constant creative awareness drove him on. His cousins would send up his food in a tin pail attached to a pulley and at times, it would come back down uneaten. When a particular part of a scene was intricate, he would not stop painting for weeks and in the darkness of night, he would paint by moonlight.

The crystalline surface of the plaster formed a glass-like consistency, fixing the color for all time; once it dried, it was absolutely permanent. He knew that its beauty would only increase with age, and, with proper protection, last for many years. Michael thought of his own mortality all the while, high up on his scaffold, and he envisioned a permanency for his family, the color of their lives, crystalline and fixed for all time, increasing in beauty with each new life.

On the surface of the high ceiling, he painted his bright-colored fresco and with the help of his cousins, mixed his stucco from gypsum, marble, dust and glue, as the Romans had been doing since ancient times. His magnificent scene of San Giovanni portrayed his village and Bella's, one on either end of the mural. They were connected in the center by the lover's bridge and the celestial whirlwind, which, with all of his skill, Michael captured faithfully. A tornado of lightening bolts and wind spirals were depicted descending from a sapphire sky, imprinting its message forever in the hearts of the couple sitting by the stream. Michael brilliantly recreated that moment in time forever. His beautiful Bella would only have to lift her chin and look upward to revisit the miracle of their meeting. When his tribute was completed, he knew she would be pleased. He had built his queen a castle and an image made of sand, which could not be washed away in the tides of time.

For six months, Michael had worked himself to exhaustion, and, when he had finished, it was a time for great rejoicing and celebrating. As a mark of respect and great love for their cousin, Lorenzo and Alberto planned a fiesta, the likes of which Sands Point had not seen. Fiona arrived with her finest cuisine. She carried baskets filled with wine and food with Miss Cornelia tagging behind her, flitting from basket to basket in ecstatic murmurings. Fiona had worked for many days to provide enough foodstuffs for Michael and his friends. Even all of Fiona's one-time boarders came to celebrate his happiness, for they too were also anxious to see what Michael had created. Throughout the festivities, they all exclaimed that this was surely one of the finest houses in all of Sands Point and reflective of Michael Guardi's genius, and the beautiful fresco on his kitchen ceiling was worthy of being compared with the Italian masters. As a tribute to Michael, his friends presented him with a watch fob, and dangling from its chain was a small golden hod. After presenting the gift, cousin Lorenzo, a man slow of speech and of few words, raised his voice to a swell in order to be heard over the large crowd and declared, "Our Michael has proved himself, in his magnificent painting, his building of mansions, and his architectural designs are worthy of his being called our new country's Renaissance Man. Are not the Alamo in Texas and the Dana House at Yale constructed of stucco?" Lorenzo's face beamed when he thought that his first oratory had received applause. He had done his homework well.

That night Michael slept peacefully for the first time in many months on his hard elevated bed, and when he awoke in the morning, his heart was full to bursting. *Now* he thought, overwhelmed with emotion, *it is time to send the fare to Bella and the children to come to America.*

CHAPTER 6

THE QUILT

Sewing seam after seam, cutting, patching, and piecing together remnants of fabric, Bella's fingers flew. She was quilting a blanket for her little Chiara, and it had to be finished before the strong winter winds blew in across the bay. Singing softly, she stitched the fresh colored squares from her discarded aprons and tablecloths. *I will leave the top of my quilt open,* she thought, *and fill it with Baa's soft fleece, that is, if she is willing to share.*

She was a Bergamasca lop-eared sheep. In the village where Bella was born, it was customary for the mother of small children to be gifted a sheep to supply her family table with milk and cheese. "What shall we name her?" she asked her toddlers. Two-year-old Gio was rolling back and forth on the ground holding his sides in fits of laughter while attempting to echo the shaky, throated *baa* of their new pet. When Bella finally understood her youngest son's unusual behavior, she said to him, "You are laughing, my serious little Gio. The sheep has awakened happiness in your soul with her sounds. We will call her 'Baa.'" From then on Baa would provide the children with milk and, at times, the milk would be made into feta or ricotta cheese and, ultimately, into Bella's famous cheese pies. But for all of that, Baa was their beloved pet.

Baa often followed Bella into Papa's olive groves, through the grape arbors and down the slope to the creek. Whenever she went into the pasture to gather flowers for her mother's devotional altar, Baa was at her heels and with her split upper lip she picked away at the preferred blossoms and dropped them into Bella's apron.

One day, a perfect afternoon for an outdoor bath, Bella, who now wore the sheepish grin, brought her faithful companion down to the creek to wash her in its cool waters. By the time Baa was clean, Bella was soaked and chilly. They dried themselves in the sun, and then Bella hoisted the little pet across her shoulders and ran to the shearing shed across the village. When they arrived, she gently put down her light burden, for she wanted Baa to walk into the shed on her own. She said softly, "My dear little sheep, you have already given your milk so generously to feed my children. Now I have another favor to ask of you: The cutter is going to shear your wool, for I need it to fill the blanket I have quilted for our Chiara. If you do this, she will be warm all through the winter. I promise the clipping will not hurt." Baa trusted Bella. She had always recognized her voice and had memorized her face. Unlike a child getting its first haircut, clinging onto the striped pole outside the barbershop, Baa did not balk. She obediently followed her mistress into the shed and submitted to the cutting without uttering a baa. When the shearing was completed, and the fleece was tossed to Bella; she caught it in her arms and with tenderness pressed it to her heart. To avoid being seen by the villagers, the two returned home by way of the creek, because, to an observer, Baa would be a sorry sight in her bare skin, her only covering one of embarrassment.

Bella boiled a large pot of water, poured it into the outdoor washing tub, and lowered in the gray fleece. After she had scrubbed it clean, she spread it out on the grass, where the strong rays of the sun bleached it as white as snow. She then skirted it with a very fine rake to remove the impurities from its merino-like wool. She slipped the finished quilt from her clothesline of rope and carefully proceeded to insulate it with the fleece. That evening when it was cool, she placed her hands over Chiara's, and, as they knelt by the child's trundle, they prayed for Papa, who was in America—the beautiful land across the ocean. Then Bella tucked her child in beneath the warmth of the soft quilt and thanked God for His love, adding a special prayer for Baa.

CHAPTER 7

PRECIOUS CARGO

They waited on the wharf with the other emigrants for the ship to take them to America. Gaetana untwisted the string tied around the small package that held her parting gift to her daughter. All the while, Bella's tears clouded her eyes, so that when her mother wound the rosary around her fingers, she could only feel the little worn beads. "I have prayed these since I was a young girl," Gaetana said. "When you pray them, I will know, and I will join my heart to yours and you will be comforted on your life's journey. Our God will be with us my Bella, for He has said, 'where two or more are gathered in My name, there am I.' He is not a breaker of promises." For over seventy years, Bella prayed on her mother's silver linked rosary, and there was not a time that she did not feel her closeness.

The steamship was pulling into harbor, and there was little time left to say their final goodbyes. Bella held her children close to her side, the quilt slipping from her arm. Gaetana caught it, and making it easier for her daughter to shepherd them onto the boat, she lifted it high over Bella's head. Billowing, it fell protectively on the young girl's shoulders. Leaning forward, she fastened it with her tin broach and as she pushed the pin through the thick padding, it pricked her finger. A drop of Gaetana's blood fell, and a small splash of red appeared on the quilt to mark the leaving.

The impact of the separation found its aim with razor sharpness. Her silent sacrifice was more than she could bear, and she futilely tried to pull them back with her eyes as they processed upward on the ramp. The strain of it produced a shrieking noise within her throat, aborted before it could be heard. She could barely make them out as they pressed forward with the other brave, bewildered souls. When she was sure they were aboard, Gaetana turned to leave, lamenting that they were no more. The weight of pain made her shoulders sag. Her chin was thick with folds as it fell upon her heaving chest and her muffled sobs went unnoticed as she walked away. With dirge-like sounds, Baa lagged stubbornly behind. In funereal procession, they headed towards their village. If you had looked closely, you could have seen Gaetana counting off her sorrowful mysteries on her fingers.

Aboard the ship, one might have thought the young girl a strange sight in her long black dress and cloak of apron remnants cascading from her shoulders. But Bella's beauty was such that her clothing was not noticed. Her skin was translucent like the white cowrie shell found on the shores of Northern Italy, and her hair as lustrous as the mystical black onyx. Her eyes were a hazel green, which matched the color of the autumn leaf caught midway in its time of changing.

Bella and her children, Alfredo, thirteen; Giovanni, eleven; and Chiara, four; traveled in steerage in the bowels of the boat, just as Michael had done. Accompanying them were Bella's two cousins traveling at Michael's behest to take protective care of his little family on the transatlantic voyage.

Their living quarters were in the tween deck, a deck below main and two decks below upper. To reach their quarters, the descent was deep and narrow, the iron ladder perpendicular and rusty. The hold was called steerage because the livestock were on the same deck as the emigrants. The bovine creatures never ceased to create a cacophony of noises that insulted their ears. A small space was assigned to them, and their family bunk was marked. Rough boards, set up to be used as beds, lined both sides of the ship. The bunks were double decked, one on top of the other. So close were they that while sitting up, the emigrants had to hunch their shoulders, and their cramped muscles would sometimes set the day's mood.

Mattresses were filled with wood chips or straw, where lice and fleas thrived and multiplied in their unsanitary habitats. The ever-present smell of seasickness hung in the stagnant air, where disease played out its malignant purpose and spread, selecting the smallest victims to infect. The narrow passage between the bunks had no ventilation other than from a hood built over the single hatch, the only entrance to their quarters. An evil foulness of the brine from the ocean seeped in and mixed with every other odor. In rough weather, the hatch was closed and the hold was as dark as night.

Due to overcrowding below, small fights would break out. When this happened, Bella would grab her children and ascend the treacherous ladder to the upper deck. Most emigrant-carrying ships did not allow steerage passengers on deck, but on this crossing, due to the unusual amount of infant deaths below, the rule was suspended by the sympathetic captain.

Bella and her children would breathe in the fresh, salty air of the ocean and gain succor from the pestilence below. Early on, she claimed her spot on deck, and not one of her fellow passengers would begrudge her this little comfort. By the railing, she would sit on a small canvas chair with her daughter on her lap. Gio and Fredo had retrieved the chair after a myopic deckhand, while attempting to fling the worn out sitter overboard, missed his mark. He left it there, imprisoned between the rail bars languishing precariously for days, awaiting reprieve. A last-minute pardon was granted when Bella's boys who, as they tugged at the wet canvas, justly won its release and triumphed over what the elements could not destroy. "Aha," Fredo cried, "a chair for Mama. It is sturdy enough for her to hold Chiara on her lap. What a wonderful find." They set it close to the railing for Mama and Chiara. Gio on one side and Fredo the other, their bodies damp and shivering, the serious little men stood guard like brave soldiers protecting their precious cargo.

The refreshing sea air often showered the little family with its salty sprays. Chiara would offer herself to its teasing, and with fits of laughter, she would squint her eyes and enjoy the game as the water surprised and cooled her sunburned face. The merciful sea spray was a different kind of game for Gio. It often saved him from shame, as it hid the tears he could no longer hold back. As the waves broke against the deck, their sound and fury were cruel confirmation of Gio's breaking heart. A deep and profound sense of aloneness would engulf his youthful spirit, and a loud crack, not unlike the snapping of a twig from its branch, could be heard in the cloudy mist above. Talking to no one at all, Gio said, "This is not my choice. My destiny has been decided for me. I will never belong in this new world of theirs." The impact of irreparable separation would be felt by Giovanni for many years to come.

Held together by the tin clasp, its luster gone, rusted by the sea air, the quilt hugged Bella's shoulders and enfolded its warmth upon her child curled up on her lap. Chiara tugged playfully at a corner of the quilt until her chubby fingers wound themselves around a small soft patch. She tilted her head and rubbed its softness on the side of her cheek. All the while, a visceral reaction to the memory of Baa permeated her tiny nostrils and filled her with the comfort of the security all children crave. Bella looked down and smiled. For a moment, her own fears were allayed, but there were times when the separation from everything she had ever known would overwhelm her, and she too, would find solace as her mother's parting gift slipped through her fingers and her fractured soul would pray for the will to go on. Her fifty Aves intoned the background music for her meditation on the life of Christ, who knew her loneliness, and again His response was swift and she was made whole again.

There were those days when the little family would remain on deck until the sun was going down over the ocean's edge. This sight filled Bella's being. As the waves quietly lapped against the ship's side, she was filled with the gentle love of God. Her strength renewed, the courageous little family would descend into the darkness and continue on their journey.

Michael had taught his son to play his mandolin at a very early age, and by the time Fredo was eight, with genius musical intelligence he had mastered the instrument. Fredo had inherited his sensitivity to sound and rhythm which was as natural as breathing for the Guardi family. Fredo's reverence for the mandolin pleased Michael and he entrusted it to his care for the voyage. At night, when enduring the indignities of the cramped sleeping quarters, he would lay its soundboard on his chest where his heart would be closer to his treasure. He remembered that before his father had left for his voyage to America, Papa had told him the story of how the mandolin had been handed down to him and how it had provided him with the liras to pay his passage. "But most of all my gratitude," he said, "is for its beautiful sounds which provided me the confidence to bend my knee and win your mother's heart." Eight-year-old Fredo was enraptured with the story of his parents meeting. Sitting at his father's feet as Papa continued gently strumming his mandolin, his pulse quickened and made him feel that he was transported in time. In years to come he would often think of that moment his father had shared his love for his mother and his heart would be filled happiness.

Michael continued with a story that Fredo never tired of hearing. "Your ancestors traveled in good company, my son.

St. Francis was also a troubadour, and he too played his lute and blessed all who had ears to hear." Michael's face always took on the radiance of an angel in the telling. With pride he remarked that the mandolin was born in Naples and was a cousin to the lute.

"I have important work to do," he said, "and I need my hod to do it. My one back has only room enough to carry my hod, and my mandolin is too dear a friend to drag rudely behind me on the journey. I leave it in your care, as you have proved yourself worthy of the honor."

Michael placed the instrument in Fredo's small lap, and as he did, his son's fingers caressed the finely carved rosettes encircling its soundboard. "I will guard this treasure with my life," he said. His father believed him and knew that his provider was in the best of hands.

Even in the bowels of the ship, Fredo was at home. When things became too much to endure for the other passengers, he played Papa's mandolin. With sweet music lifting them above their mental anguish, the horrific conditions surrounding the emigrants were soon forgotten. The thirteen-year-old boy in him soon became a man, as he denied himself while serving others. Blessed with Michael's loving disposition, he went from bunk to bunk where typhoid spread quickly in their confining quarters. Most affected were the infants, victims of the ship owners who greedily crammed their ships with too many passengers and cattle, making the voyage dangerous and unhealthy. Because their love of money overruled their reason, the most vulnerable passengers were denied their right to live. With tenderness, Fredo would play his mandolin and as they breathed their last, their little souls would become one with the brilliant harmonies and ascend into the highest realms of glory.

THE CASTLE

The long and arduous journey had come to an end. The Guardi family separation was now a thing of the past. As the Victorian pulled into port, Bella and the three children leaned over the railing and waved excitedly, for they had spotted Michael on the pier. He looked much older now. The five years of separation and unremitting hard labor had contributed to his aging and had taken its toll on his boyish good looks but nothing could diminish his radiant appearance, for his family had come home.

Still tired from their journey, they arrived at Sands Point exhausted, but all the sufferings of the months at sea had soon been forgotten upon seeing Michael and the castle he had built for them. They were overwhelmed as they approached the mansion and could not believe what their eyes were telling them.

The first thing Michael did upon entering the estate was to lead his family up the spiral staircase and into the children's rooms. After warm baths and prayers, they were tucked in under soft quilts and each forehead was tenderly kissed good night.

It was now time for Michael to take Bella's hand and lead her down to her kitchen to show her the fresco he had painted, exemplifying their love. She was so strongly moved with emotion when she looked up and saw what he had created that she sat down on the cool tiled floor and sobbed. He knew that his masterpiece had worked its intended rapture in Bella's heart.

CHAPTER 8

MCGUFFEY'S
ONE-ROOM SCHOOLHOUSE

Behind the Guardi home on Main Street was a one-room schoolhouse. On a brisk autumn morning, Bella awakened her little Chiara early, for she wanted to give herself enough time to prepare her only daughter for her first day of school. She brushed her long lustrous black hair and fingered it into curls. Careful not to disturb the child's crowning glory, she slipped the white organdy dress over her head, the finest Sears catalogue had to offer. When Bella was satisfied with her labor of love, she called to Michael to come and see their beautiful daughter.

Chiara tried to look brave as she stood on her toes to stretch her height and reached up to pat her mother's shoulder. Bella's sighs and quivering lips betrayed her feelings as her only daughter walked slowly away, and after a very few halting steps, Chiara turned her head to see her mother sobbing in the doorway.

Michael ached to give his daughter every advantage their new country had to offer. He knew that learning the language was the key to her assimilation. Being discriminate with his vocabulary, he never used the phrase "melting pot," as so many of his friends had. "We will mix in," he had told his family more than once. In spite of this distinction, only Italian was spoken in the home, so consequently Chiara had no knowledge of her adopted country's language. To reassure him that the timing was right for Chiara, for she was only five and in his mind a baby still, he turned and in Italian he loudly proclaimed to Bella who was still at the back door wiping her eyes on her apron: "It is time for our Chiara to become an Americana." With that, he held more tightly to his daughter's hand as they walked across the backyard and into the arms of opportunity. In order to enter the schoolyard, they had to squat down to maneuver the almost impenetrable foliage separating the two properties. In the process, Chiara laughed and clapped her hands, amused at the sight of Papa's undignified plight, for she loved this new game they were playing. Parting the bushes, the two collaborators approached the "house of learning."

Miss Cornelia, teacher and librarian, stood on the porch of the one-room schoolhouse and rang the bell. From every direction, eager students came running to the toll, and some not so eager, for their unwashed ears were too clogged with dirt to hear the magic spell the bell was casting. Through her small round spectacles, the bell ringer looked down her nose and perceived the rustling of branches. She was shocked to see Michael in such an awkward pose, bending low and separating the hedge, and her eyes widened but, with prophetic insight, she proclaimed yet another profound lesson to her habitually unimpressed students: "He stoops to conquer!" she exclaimed. Michael's growing reputation commanded more respect than he was now displaying and she recognized him at once. She had attended the celebration for the completion of his house and when she recalled his magnificent kitchen-ceiling masterpiece, she marveled at his genius. Prissily pursing her lips, she nodded self-approval, taking partial credit for the influence she must have had on his artistic enterprise. It was necessary to be free of anxiety when one was creative, she thought. Didn't she provide the antidote for Michael's homesickness with her research on the game of bocce?

As father and daughter approached, she was taken in by the little girl who was glowing with infectious enthusiasm. Chiara introduced herself in her native language and her pronunciation was perfection. Melodic oval shapes tones rolled over her lips and made pleasant contact with Cornelia's overly trained ear. From that day on, five-year-old Chiara trotted through her backyard, at times scratching her legs on freshly trimmed brambles, hurrying to get to school before the bell. Nothing would deter her from her love of learning. The spinster teacher doted on her little student and was unable to resist a puff of pride when others mentioned her name with unrestrained praise.

The dedicated mentor taught Chiara reading, writing, arithmetic and grammar from the McGuffey Readers, the most effective teaching program in the country. When she had completed the first five Readers, she was ready for the sixth, which stressed the art of elocution. Miss Cornelia was experienced as an elocutionist, as she taught from "McGuffey's New Juvenile Speakers," available to the advanced pupils in every school in the country. Her obsessive need to impart her elocutionary expertise culminated in Chiara's exacting enunciation, resulting in its being almost too much for the everyday world. Many years later, her nieces, Sophia and Gina, would agree that Zia Chiara, early on, had been given one lesson too many from her zealous teacher. Her enunciation had the affected tone of the intellectual elite, but since her voice was natural to her and not put on, it allowed her access to many cultural opportunities which might otherwise have passed her by.

Miss Cornelia had instilled in her pupil a love for reading, and when she was six, she presented Chiara with her own library card. Not content to borrow books, Chiara begged the librarian to let her help out with the stack still haphazardly heaped in the corner of the class room. Now, the books were higher than when Fiona had visited due to donations from the more affluent locals. After arranging them in neat piles, with all the concentration a six-year-old could muster, Chiara sat cross-legged on the floor, stamp pad in hand. Taking her job seriously, her little forehead pruned with a sense of responsibility when anyone approached her "office." Delicate little fingers were often smudged black from the ink on the stamping pad and her organdy dresses were ever a challenge for Bella's washboard, but neither mother nor daughter seemed to mind. Her very first job was pounding out the due dates on homemade cardboard cards. She could never have imagined that one day she would be the head librarian of the most prestigious library on the Island, and that her fifty years of tenure would be on these very premises.

Within a year of Chiara entering school, Bella gave birth to twin girls. They were christened at St. Peter's and given the names Guglielmina and Philomena. The following year, she and Michael were blessed with infant Rosa, who was not destined to survive for long. Chiara's joy at the arrival into her life of her twin sisters and infant Rosa, brought out the maternal instincts common to little girls. She would spend endless days enchanting them with her voice as she read them nursery rhymes from her library books. They lived in a world filled with wonder and their lives were complete.

Guglielmina and Philomena spent their second birthday in their shared trundle bed. Throughout the day, Bella and six-year-old Chiara each took a little one in their arms and sat with them in the rocking chairs. It soothed and comforted them, and from time to time, the babies would nod off. Whenever they were put down again, they would soon fretfully awaken. Chiara would tuck Baa's blanket under their tiny chins and reasoned they would be soothed and find the comfort it had always given her and soon they would be "all better".

When her brothers returned from school and Papa from work and they passed the nursery, they, too, were filled with great concern. It was the worst of times in the little hamlet by the water. An epidemic of waterborne cholera came into all of the homes and touched the lives of every family in town. Bella's two little girls were not exempt from the plague and even with all of the medication available; their little bodies were not strong enough to fight off the fatal disease. Bella and Chiara stayed the night by their bedside and by morning, there was stillness in the nursery. Guglielmina and Philomena had awakened with the angels, and before the month was over, the sleeping place in the churchyard had opened its earthy portal for the second time and infant Rosa joined her sisters.

The severe shock of the unexpected separation would haunt Chiara and her family for many years.

After a time, Chiara found great solace in her books and prayed that one day she would travel and visit all of the countries she had been reading about. When her primary and secondary education was completed, she attended a woman's college across the country. For an Italian family, the idea of a daughter leaving the home to go so far away to school was not a consideration, but resolute Chiara persisted, and finally Bella and Michael reluctantly conceded.

CHAPTER 9

ARBOR DAYS

Back in Naples, the grape arbor had been intrinsically woven into the everyday lives of the families of Bella and Michael. The grapes were used for their table wine and for making jam. The shaded arbor was an outdoor room where they enjoyed most of their meals. It was also the meeting place with friends and neighbors and the center of all of their social activity. For Michael, nothing would do but to add this essential extension onto their American home.

With an artisan's skill, he laid the tile for the patio surrounding the arbor. So beautiful were his results that it became its focal point. The arbor consisted of four sides and a roof of sturdy, interlocking steel wires, so that in season, as the plump, heavy-laden clusters ripened, they would be safe on their vines until harvested. Then Gio and Fredo would fill baskets to overflowing and carry them down to Papa in his wine cellar.

After the grapes were pressed and made into wine for the family table, Michael took the residue of skins, stems, and seeds, and fermented them in wooden casks to make grappa. His creation was soft and delicate to the taste, with the strong aroma of the grape. Next, he stored it in oaken casks. On holidays, Bella would spout the golden liquid into her crystal decanter and serve it as a digestive after one of her five-course meals. After dinner, she would cautiously pour a small amount of grappa into each demitasse of espresso. The drink created was called "caffe corratto," or corrected coffee. Because the grappa was fermented in wooden barrels for a few years, the grappa turned an irresistible amber color, enticing the palate. But since Papa's brandy was 120 proof, too much grappa would result in too festive a holiday. For many years, Papa played his mandolin after dinner. As time passed and Papa's hands became too palsied, his "provider" was passed on to his exceptionally talented son.

CHAPTER 10

GIO, ANOTHER KIND OF ARTIST

In the overcrowded one-room schoolhouse, his tall frame dominated the classroom, which made him look older than his classmates. Giovanni began his schooling in his new country by not fitting in. He had more inches than grace, and from then on, he used his height to his own advantage.

The family called him Gio. Thick black hair, trimmed just enough to give him a casual look, curled around his handsome face, which masked his serious persona. It was no secret that he was the black sheep of the family and consequently was tortured by his younger cousins, who tormented him with sing–song childishness. They would intone Baa Baa Black Sheep and taunt in Italian, "Why don't you melt in the pot the way we do?" and Gio would stiffen his neck, throw back his head as he strutted before his tormentors, and yell back, "If you're all so assimilated, why don't you taunt me in English?"

By the time Gio was sixteen, he had entered into a prison of his own making and lashed out at everyone who displeased him. This turned out to be more a curse for him than for his unsuspecting victims.

His fuse was getting shorter, and his temper flared with more frequency. "It was not my choice to come to this country. I do not belong here, I want to leave," he said to anyone who would listen. When he could no longer stand his world of separation, he decided to run away. Gio gave no thought of breaking his mother's heart. He reasoned that he was now a man, and his mother should expect nothing less than that her Gio was going out into the world to make his way. Yet, his love for her was the only emotion he was capable of feeling, and even for someone as unconscionable as Gio, the parting caused him great pain. It would turn out to be a heavy-weighted journey, as he was taking with him years of baggage too burdensome for him to carry. As the wanderlust urged him on, Gio habitually walked into brick walls, hardening his heart, as well as his head. From time to time, he would call his mother, but for the next ten years, he was much too busy sidestepping the law.

Giulia was cleaning Gio's table at a free lunch bar when he noticed her. It was her dark, earthy beauty that caught his eye, and serious Gio surprised himself and smiled at her.

The barmaid lived in a seedy boarding house nearby, and Gio had been looking for a cheap room. Encouraged by her obvious interest in him, he followed her to her shabby dwelling and rented a room down the hall. After a two-week courtship, they were married.

Within a year a son was born. "I shall call him Americo," Gio told Giulia, "after our *Pisano* who discovered this country. Maybe he will find it easier to fit in than I did. It was on that wretched boat coming over, as the ocean divided the two continents, that I first suffered the separation from my homeland."

His envy of those who had come from the old country and adapted, and even prospered, gnawed at his soul. He felt that he had nothing to be thankful for. "If you were here, sister Chiara,"

Gio chuckled, "in your high-toned voice you would admonish me with one of your Shakespearian quotes as you so often did in the old days. 'Sharper than a serpent's tooth is an ungrateful child, Gio,' you would say. "I guess that's me, all right."

Staring down at the little stranger in its unadorned orange crate on the floor, Gio interrupted his trend of thought when the big orange letters stamped on the side of the crate caught his eye. "Maybe I should have called you Florida. I was being right generous giving you the name of your country, making it a smoother sell for you to swindle your countrymen." Gio, with all the bitterness of a cynic, decided that he would pass on to his son the dark side of his own unholy mission in life, the things that gave him most satisfaction: his inordinate desire to have what belonged to others, and his insatiable greed. Unwittingly, breaking these commandments had a special appeal to the young boy in Gio. Now, however, it was time for them to leave their shabby room. The rent was due.

CHAPTER 11

THE RULE

The sun had not yet risen, and ten-year-old Rico was still half asleep, shivering more from fear than cold. He stood alone on the front steps of a low, grey building in the middle of nowhere. His father, Giovanni, and mother, Giulia, had worn out their welcome with the Guardi family and had no contact with them for many years. Asking them to take on their little problem wasn't an option. Giovanni and Guilia had had enough of parenting, and Rico was becoming a burden; he didn't fit in with their wanton lifestyle. They wanted to be free of their only son and did the unpardonable and dropped him off at an orphanage like a sack of potatoes. Telling Rico that they would be back in a week or two, the boy had little hopes of them keeping their promise. Early on, he had learned to be suspicious with trusting these people who had given him life.

Attempting to feel a sense of balance, he dug his feet into the soggy mat on the porch, and with shoulders hunched; he whispered to himself, "I'm not a baby in a blanket to be dropped off like this." Embarrassment spread through his body inundating him with waves of nausea. He had experience with successfully escaping humiliating situations in the past, and with a shift of his mind, he entered into a state of his own alternate reality where, momentarily, he found relief.

Rico's slack jaw and detached demeanor made him appear stupid. In his weakened state, a few light raps on the door were all he could muster. His feeble knocking finally fell on the ears of the orphanage director who was on his way out of the squalid building. Intimidated when he saw Rico's tall frame dominating the doorway and feeling inferior because of his own very small statue, he spit out a dismissive aside through his tobacco stained teeth. "Get lost kid. Whatever you're selling, we're not buying any." Stuttering badly, the young boy said, "I'm Rico and my folks said you'd take me in. They'll be back to pick me up in a week or two." "Yeah, I've heard that before." Sizing up the potential in this newcomer, he reconsidered. "Don't just stand there, dummy, we just got another vacancy." He chuckled to himself, recalling the brutal fate of his latest disciplinary disaster, and said sarcastically "When you learn the ropes and get a little older, we'll need another orphan on the cobblers' bench, little man."

Rico wanted to explain again that he really did have parents but knew his words would fall on deaf ears. His lobes were burning from being pulled along by the director as he was dragged down a darkened hallway and shoved into a small cell of a room. When he saw the sheet-less cot and bared windows, he cried aloud, "Am I in a jail?" Sobbing, Rico sat on the edge of the bed. He slumped down and put his head in his hands as his body trembled underneath his cloak of pain.

The weeks went by and turned into years. Rico's development had already been arrested at the early age of ten when he stood alone on the porch of the orphanage. As his teenage years dragged by in menial servitude, he at last had the long-awaited, dubious distinction of being selected to work at the cobbler's bench repairing shoes for the townspeople.

This is where Rico met his new friend. Joey had been at the orphanage since birth and had known no other life. He explained to Rico that there was one rule, which if not obeyed, would have horrible consequences. The rule was that they were not allowed to use any of the materials in the shop to mend their own shoes. They shod their feet with leftovers from the shoe bin in the hall, shoes that were beyond mending. If they were lucky and beat the other boys to the bin, there might be a matching pair, and if the shoes were too small or too large, it was better than none at all. They would stuff them with paper or squeeze them onto their sorry feet.

By the time Joey turned eighteen, his innate feelings of right from wrong had taken hold and he became deeply troubled. He could no longer stomach the culmination of a lifetime of abuse, and the injustices and outright brutality by the wardens became intolerable. More deeply aware that the wardens were without conscience, the rude awakening traumatized him. This epiphany would force him, out of desperation, to take action.

No one at the cobbler's bench had to guess that Rico had been to the charity bin when the noise from his shoes announced his arrival. Flip, flop was the all too familiar sound throughout the small room. Both body and sole of the worn out covering Rico was wearing were separating, for they were held together by a string and a prayer. Joey had found his moment. He bent over Rico, put a hand on his shoulder, and spoke loud enough for all the boys in the cobbler shop to hear.

"I will mend your charity shoes for you, my friend, and I do this knowing that I will be punished." With that, he knelt and gently slipped the shoes from Rico's feet and inched one over the plate on the sewing machine. With a whir, the shuttle fed the bobbin as it rose and fell on the cause of Joey's despair. No sooner had he made the first stitch, than the warden loomed up behind him.

"Gotcha" he shrieked, and hauled Joey out to the yard. A shiver swept through the boys on the bench and some sobbed, because the rule had been broken. Rico grabbed a stool and set it under a small window that was high up near the ceiling. He had to stretch to reach the dingy pane and using his shirtsleeve, he rubbed hard and cleared a spot, only to be horrified at what he saw happening to Joey in the yard below. That one glance sickened him. His friend was being beaten so violently by the insane warden that Rico fell off the stool and lay on the floor too stunned to move. When he could get to his feet, he was unable to think clearly. In a panic, he ripped his unsown shoe from its metal plate, breaking the needle in two. Another infraction of the rule ran through Rico's mind. *I will surely die,* he thought, and with that in mind, he headed for the highway.

After a few miles of walking on the hard surfaced road, the cardboard, which had been stuffed into the soles of his shoes, had worn away. His feet were hot and burning, and bulbs of ripe blisters popped up in between his toes. The flip-flopping became louder with no cobbler boys around to hear or care. Rico felt very alone. As an omen of things to come, the body and sole were now completely detached. He gave a thought to why Joey would risk his life for a few stitches, but then the thought went as fast as it came and evaporated in the morning mist. "I have no need of these anymore," he said, and tossed the ominous symbols of his future into a nearby ditch. Rico continued barefoot without a backward glance. When he reached town, he headed for the shoe store, and cutting through the back door screen, he entered and stole the first pair of brand new shoes he had ever owned. With his new shoes, Rico felt that he could walk on water.

CHAPTER 12

FALL FROM GRACE

Rico continued on his journey, tricking his way through life with smoke and mirrors, but as his sense of self hit rock bottom, he flirted with the idea that he was entitled to help himself to the earnings of others. He harbored the thought that he was owed big, and that small time stuff was a thing of the past. He became an entitlement addict, a consummate con man. Once his craft was well honed, he planned to deceive on a larger scale. For many years, this seed, which had rooted in his soul, grew until it became a festering boil. When it came to a head and broke, it burst forth its green seepage of envy, and its wickedness suffocated his soul.

Up until now, the greed to which Rico subjected himself was a symptom of his disease, but an insidious change had been progressing slowly since his escape from the orphanage. He was on a slippery slide, exhilarated in the momentum of the spiral plunge that rewarded him by dumping him into a bottomless pit. The chasm was so deep that he was puzzled when he found his soul curiously uninhabited. Unable to grasp at truth, the lie he was about to embark upon completely enveloped him in an unholy mixture of the strange fire of greed and envy. Rico became his own god.

CHAPTER 13

ST. PETER'S

When they vacationed with her each summer, Chiara would take Gina, Sophia, and Carlo to Saint Peter's Church for Mass on Sundays. They would all kneel in the front pew, mesmerized by the choir voices coming from the loft. There were times when the congregation was blessed with the beautiful voice of parish member, singer Perry Como, whose faith and service was not as well known to the general public. Everyone's voices soared to the rafters in accompaniment. It was at this church many years before that Grandma Bella had also worshiped. Each morning, hand in hand, she and Chiara would walk over the small, green wooden bridge that connected her home to God's. It always reminded her of the bridge connecting her village to Michael's in the old country.

On the corner of Main Street, with its spires rising up majestically to the heavens, was the Church of St. Peter. Its magnificent architectural design was unique and distinctive. On an infinitely smaller scale, with great pride, the more traveled residents compared it to the Sagrada Familia in Barcelona, Spain. Here Bella and her only daughter would patiently wait on the steps for the sexton to open the doors for morning Mass, and for mother and daughter it was like entering the threshold of heaven.

CHAPTER 14

BELLA'S WAKE

The name Isabella means, "to be consecrated to God,"; and in truth, to her family, she was a saint.

It was the mid 1900s, a time when wakes in Italian families were mostly endured in the home. The family was all gathered together to say their last goodbyes to Grandma Bella. She was laid out in the living room surrounded by lavish displays of glorious white lilies, a sharp contrast to the sea of black surrounding her. Alfredo's children, teenagers Sophia, Gina, and Carlo, were the only grandchildren at the time and were required to attend. They arrived totally unprepared for what was about to happen.

Upon entering the house, they noticed that wafting in and out and emerging from the wall were barely discernable outlines of dark shadowy figures. When these phantoms began to vocalize, the children were visibly shaken. Little women in black dresses and head shawls lined the perimeter of the room. Actually, they were neighbors and friends of the family who were the official mourners for the occasion. They were hired to fan the fires of grief out of respect for the departed. It was and outward sign of sorrow, although to the uninformed it would seem to indicate that the family was "buying tears."

This was a practice that went back to the middle ages, when the early Romans hired criers, and in some societies, even today, the custom still remains. In most countries, women were hired for this unusual distinction, as they were considered hardwired to display more of an ability to feel loss. No one had thought to explain beforehand these orchestrated outbursts to the grandchildren. Whenever the doleful rhythm would start up, their dewy eyes widened and their innocent hearts, like fluttering birds, almost leapt out of their rib cages. What happened next compounded their shock. An attempt to revive Grandma occurred when she was lifted from her satin-lined bed. This stirring act of repentant sorrow by Gio was quickly corrected, but not before leaving its indelible mark on their youthful psyches.

When they were properly traumatized, their shaky little legs were marched in lock step with the elders, as they processed to Heaven's Gate Cemetery across town. Stoically the criers took the lead in this extraordinary parade. Four abreast and four deep, their long, black skirts swept the dirt roads, creating clouds of dust in their wake. Sideline watchers viewed this sight with heightened curiosity, and when the moaning reached a fever pitch, it was evident that they were taking their job seriously. Their numbers indicated to the observers that this must be a prosperous family, for in those times, this was not only acceptable but also sought after as a sign of devotion and respect for the departed member of the family.

As they approached graveside, things really began to heat up. By now, the children's sensitivities were numbed. What was about to happen would pierce the emotional recesses of their dignity: Losing his footage, Giovanni had also lost his mental balance, and Alfredo had to restrain him from jumping into the open grave to retrieve dear Grandma. He was overpowered by guilt when he realized too late just how he had wounded his mother's heart. In desperate need for her forgiveness, he sobbed out his mea culpa. The impression that this scene left on the bewildered grandchildren paralyzed them with fear. So much so, that when many years later Uncle Gio passed away and they again were required to attend the funeral, they were terrified. They knew that going to the graveside would trigger off emotions best left alone. Their only recourse was to get on their knees and pray. They made their partitioning pilgrimage to St. Peter's, bowed their heads, and prayed for all they were worth. The kneeler was kinder now, for in the passing of time, their bony knees had filled out and provided the padding, unlike when they were younger and hard bone met hard wood.

As they drove through the tall arches of Heaven's Gate Cemetery, their anxious souls were calmed. With Divine Compassion, the Lord of all Mercy answered their desperate pleadings by giving them a peace that went beyond their understanding.

Sixty years had passed since the angels of light and thunderbolts had joined the souls of Bella and Michael. Only a few lonely months had elapsed before Grandpa Michael took his final leap of faith and crossed the bridge between heaven and earth and joined his love forever.

Forthcoming events, which had cast their shadows before them, fulfilled Gio's destiny at his own passing. His mea culpa at long last had found favor. His desperate attempt at atonement that he had demonstrated years before was realized when he was buried in the same grave with his mother and father.

CHAPTER 15

CHIARA'S WORLD

Early on, one of Chiara's fellow librarians entered her life in a permanent way. Newell was a stub of a man, pudgy with cushioned ribs. What he lacked in appearance he made up for in his intellect and wit. Sharing over sixty years of devoted friendship, he was heartbroken when he was unable to help her on that fatal day when her life was in mortal danger.

Chiara chose to avoid what she considered the vicissitudes of wedded bliss. She lived alone but led a full and interesting life surrounded by many friends. Her accomplishments were legendary. She founded the Crows Nest Art Community and was curator of her own Guardi Gallery, a jewel of Italian architecture set in the heart of downtown Sands Point. Her avid appetite for the arts often took her to Rome where she selected rare works of art for her preeminent collection at the gallery. Her quest would always begin with a visit to the village of her mother's youth. Here, she would feel close to Nona Gaetana and Nono Paulo when she visited and prayed at their sleeping place in the grove, nestled under the peach trees.

In the entrance hall of Chiara's gallery, majestically hanging high above from its vaulted ceiling was the symbol of everything the Guardi family embraced. It was a heraldic banner dramatizing the embodiment of sacrifice and service with the fleece of a sheep inside the many patches from Bella's aprons. Its message was simple and powerful, conveying the significance of real life, and because of this it was considered a fine work of art. Anyone entering the impressive entrance portal and creating the slightest breeze would cause the banner to sway back and forth on its rod, filling the aficionados with a sense of wonder for what was awaiting them within. A small splash of red still permeating its fabric could be seen by those pausing to appreciate its familial implication.

Chiara had the joy of launching many local artists' careers and generously gave them the opportunity to display and sell their works of art at the gallery. The artists had no need to go any further than their own Sands Point coastal landscape, a playground of unbelievable natural beauty, in order to create their magnificent land and seascapes on canvas. With hundreds of mansions and the who's who of high society in the vicinity with old money, the artists, with the passion of the zealots, were kept painting at their easels at a feverishly high speed. After expanding the gallery, Chiara hosted many other cultural activities. She often featured juried exhibitions composed of a selection committee where local craftsmen submitted their artwork for judging.

Chiara was ecstatic when Fredo gave freely of his talent when called upon to do benefit concerts for the local children's hospital. She was more than proud to introduce her brother as one of the foremost classical guitarists of the day.

She traveled about the world and her favorite ports of call were Egypt, Africa, and Rome. Her passion for travel, unfortunately, did not allay an indefinable restlessness, which failed to bring her to a place of true belonging in her unrequited searchings.

When she passed on, the next generation of Guardi's were there to perpetuate Michael's dream. The Guardi name had already become synonymous with art, for Michaels's fame had been long been established. He had paved the way for his uniquely talented family with his superb mosaic tile artistry and uniquely designed Tuscan styled mansions. But most of all, it was his masterpiece, "The Bridge," his fresco painted on Bella's kitchen ceiling, which brought him the most acclaim. Art critics came from abroad to examine the pinnacle of Michael's artistic achievement and all attested to the fact that this was truly the masterpiece of a genius.

When Gina and Sophia inherited the Guardi Gallery, Sophia was appointed to the curatorial position and immediately began to build on Chiara's foundation. She provided responsible leadership and walked boldly in her aunt's footsteps. Traveling abroad, she selected, interpreted, and purchased works of art, sculptures, and drawings, but a whole spectrum of prints was Gina's field of expertise. The gallery was the perfect showcase for her highly acclaimed watercolors, which she painted on many different mediums. Applying the watercolors came easy to Gina, for her personality, as with her paintings, was not controlling or dominating. Because of her ability to achieve this freedom of form, which was active in all of her paintings, the prestigious art community of the North Shore and colorists throughout the country anticipated her exhibits with great enthusiasm. To enable public access to Gina's works, the sisters designed and dedicated a print study room within the gallery for Gina's solo showings.

CHAPTER 16

THE AMERICANA

It was Gina, Sophia and Carlo's mother, who saved the day for Grandfather Michael. When Alfredo married Margaret, the dreams of Bella and Michael came to fruition. She was the one who would enable their cultural assimilation to be a certainty in their lives. Their handsome Alfredo had married the most beautiful "Americana," Margaret. The truth of the matter was that Margaret was also first generation American of Scottish and French descent. Margaret's father, James Fulton, had emigrated from Cambusnethon, Scotland, and her mother, Bernadette, from Alsace Lorraine in France.

Carlo was the first grandchild to be born in America, and when he was two weeks old, he was baptized at St. Peter's. To mark the occasion, a grand celebration for the first grandson was held. Every member of the family attended, except Gio. He could not be found. Had they searched a street corner on Park Avenue in New York City, they would have found Gio at another kind of christening. He could be seen standing in a doorway waiting for a downpour to baptize high class New Yorkers, upon which occasion he would jump out and sell them cheap umbrellas at ridiculously high prices.

There was no way of getting around it; the Guardi's offspring arrived by twos in every generation. A year after the family heralded Carlo's arrival, Fredo and Margaret were blessed with twins, Sophia and Gina. They came bringing great joy and consolation to the hearts of Grandmother Bella and Aunt Chiara, lifting their burden of many years.

Fredo began his career by playing Papa's mandolin at many celebrations, as Michael had done in Naples. With natural progression, he went on to master the classical guitar. With great passion, he studied the "method" of Florentine Mateo Carcassi, one of the greatest guitarists of the nineteenth century.

This proved to be very valuable for Fredo, for when it was discovered that he was of the same caliber as Carcassi, Fredo was acclaimed as a virtuoso concert guitarist. With intensity, he followed his idol's path and won raves in the greatest concert halls of Paris and London. Combined with a romantic soul like Papa's, he rose to unbelievable heights in his profession.

As Fredo prospered, he moved his family into the Essex House on Central Park South in New York City, which enabled him to be closer to Carnegie Hall where he mesmerized his audiences when he was not on tour. Being over thirty miles from the family on Long Island, their visits were limited to vacations and holidays.

When his children visited their grandparents and Aunt Chiara on their annual summer vacations, they felt as if they were transported to another planet. Each year they had to familiarize themselves again with old world Italian customs. Aunt Chiara customarily would seat them at the long wooden table under the cool purple canopy of the arbor to serve their meals. Her specialty was ground meat cooked and layered with olives, peppered tomatoes, and eggplant, topped off with melted provolone. This savory concoction was then wrapped in grape leaves from the arbor. When she laughingly told them that they weren't required to eat the leaves, their eyes teared up in gratitude.

The succulent melon from Great Aunt Generosa's patch complimented the gelato, which soothed their burning throats. Bella's homemade pasta was often served for dinner and was considered by all as the best rigatoni this side of Naples. It was scored, and the ridged grooves on the pasta would catch the peppered red gravy that would explode on their palates like Fourth of July sidewalk firecrackers. To wash it all down, the wine Grandfather Michael had distilled in the cellar was served as their meal beverage. Although it was watered down, when their Mama Margaret found out about this mild imbibing, she strongly disagreed with the family custom, and the age-old tradition disappeared from sight.

There came a time when Michael's normally thriving business began to have great difficulties with its cash flow. He had over-extended himself by investing heavily in property, not only on the North Shore but on the South Shore as well. In need of capital to pay the taxes on the family estate, he turned to Margaret, the business head of the family who was comptroller of Fredo's financial empire. She gave Michael the finances needed, and by doing so saved the family home. Since her children would eventually inherit most of the estate, it was not only a kind but also a wise decision.

With the passing of Bella and Michael, the existing will divided the estate among Chiara, Fredo and Gio. When the time arrived for settling the estate, hungry Gio sat at the groaning board in the kitchen, anxious to "take the money and run." With a flourish of his pen, he hastily signed the document that legalized the trade of his inheritance for a small porridge bowl of instant cash. Fredo, not in any hurry to settle the estate, decided to let things stand, and that will was never probated.

RITA SANTANIELLO MCGUFFEY

These circumstances allowed Chiara to continue living in the family home, and the interest on the family holdings were subsequently invested in the Guardi Gallery. Chiara, with her brother's approval, had a new will drawn, which stipulated that she was in ownership of all of Papa Michael's holdings, including the Gallery and house, until her demise, at which time-the heirs, Gina, Sophia, Carlo and Rico, her nieces and nephews, were to divide the estate equally.

CHAPTER 17

CORA FROM COLUMBIA

The power of Chiara's mind had not yet gone. Her vigor waned, but her spirit was very much alive. Friends would come daily to visit, and tea would be served out on the open veranda where Chiara still critiqued the paintings of up-and-coming local artists. She enjoyed the friendship of Newell and of her dwindling circle of friends. Her life was still full and productive. Although she could no longer walk, a wheel-chair took the place of her crippled legs.

Needing someone to assist her in moving about and to dispel her loneliness, divine providence intervened one summer's day and a young Columbian woman appeared on her doorstep, no one was certain from where, to be her companion and aide. Cora appeared without references. The family was concerned about that little detail, but judging backgrounds had no place in Chiara's world of no boundaries and so the stranger was warmly welcomed into her life.

Still concerned about Auntie's new companion, the family discovered, after careful investigation, that Cora had been smuggled out a few months earlier from the Andean city of Bogota, Columbia, the overland gateway to South America. It was at the time of the Violenicios, when a very uncivil war was being fought. Three hundred thousand people were murdered at the beginning of the revolution when the government regained power. Cora and her family were caught in the crossfire of the deadly violence between the right militants and the liberals. When her husband, Gabriel, was murdered in the insurrection, she frantically left her mother with her infant daughter and eventually wound up on the shores Sands Point.

No one knew for sure what her connections were back in Columbia, but Chiara welcomed her into her home on faith alone. Cora had been educated at the Columbian University and was proficient in the English language. "If only it weren't for a certain white powder and the violence, Columbia would be a paradise," she would say to Chiara, who marveled at her directness. Life was slower and the culture laid-back in Bogota, which instilled in the aide a peaceful demeanor, so vital for her elderly patient.

Within days of their first meeting, Cora had moved into the newly decorated second story suite of rooms. In lieu of rent for the accommodation, Cora happily reciprocated the kindness by doing household chores and much needed assistance. She shopped at the open markets on the waterfront and wheeled her mistress to her weekly doctor visits, and on their return home, they would lunch at Chiara's favorite restaurant, "Fiona's Daughters," in the old building still standing at the end of Main Street by the waterfront. In short order, these two unlikely souls depended upon each other for companionship, and with natural progression their fondness for each other turned into a loving mother-daughter relationship.

When Cora confessed that she had a five-year-old daughter still in Columbia, Chiara eagerly agreed to pay the child's passage and welcomed the beautiful child into her home. As with her first schoolteacher, Miss Cornelia, who had befriended her many years before, she now befriended little Nina. She doted on the little dark-haired girl, for she saw herself in the child. The connection was inevitable. She, too, had been a five-year-old foreigner in a new world. She arranged to have Nina attend private school and taught her English from her own well-worn McGuffey Readers. The roles soon became reversed and Nina would run and retrieve a book from the lower shelves in the home library and proceed to read to her "grandmother" from one of the children's books, many of which were authored by Chiara. Everything that she had ever hoped for had now come to pass and it seemed that her new family would go on forever.

Chiara's wish was to die in her own home, the home her father had built for her mother and where she had lived all of her life. In her ninety-second year, all of her needs were being met. Of her own accord, she would never have left her relatives or her newly found family.

CHAPTER 18

NIGHT OF THE GOLDEN ROSARY

Bella prayed on her mother's rosary daily, the worn beads Gaetana had wound around her fingers the day she had left Italy. It had seen her through her darkest days. When her two-year-old twins, followed so soon by her infant daughter , passed so suddenly, her beads were never at rest.

The year was 1988. Gina and Sophia had just returned from a pilgrimage to Medjugorje in Yugoslavia, where apparitions of the Blessed Virgin were being reported. While there, the links of the silver chains on their rosaries hadn't turned to gold, and they were actually surprised. Millions of pilgrims had experienced this mysterious phenomenon during the seven years the Blessed Virgin had been appearing, and theirs had not.

Father Giacomo had not gone with his mother and aunt on pilgrimage, but while they were gone, he visited a shrine in upstate New York where, in procession with other pilgrims, he climbed a small hill. Arriving at the top, they prayed before the Statue of Our Lady Queen of Peace. Kneeling before the statue and looking down at the rosary in his hand, Giacomo suddenly discovered that the links of his rosary, which were previously silver, had changed and now had a lustrous golden patina. On the next visit to his mother, Sophia asked him if he thought hers would also change if she placed her beads next to his. Giacomo smiled and said "You can try, mother." Placing the rosaries side by side on the living room table, she retired. The next morning, Sophia flew down the stairs to see if the miraculous had happened. There they were, where she had placed them, but now instead of sterling silver, they were glowing with the same golden luster as on Giacomo's beads.

That day, Sophia and Gina called their prayer group together for a night of thanksgiving. When the group arrived, one after another showed the community what also had happened that day. Everyone was blessed to have this incredible marvel imbedded into the chains of their rosaries. Gina and Sophia called Zia Chiara, who was now in her eighties, and told her of the miraculous events. They asked her if her grandmother Gaetana's rosary chain had changed as well. Chiara immediately went to her mother Bella's altar. The rosaries that grandmother Gaetana had given her mother were now over one hundred years old. Just the day before, when she fingered them, the silver chain was dark green and rusted and rough to the touch. When Charia looked down she was awe struck: the chain was now silky smooth and golden.

So overjoyed was she that in spite of her eighty years and the long distance to Sophia's house, she knew she had to attend the night of the golden Rosary celebration and share her miracle. She called cousin Beto who lived nearby and asked him to drive her to Sophia's. "Great Grandmother Gaetana's rosaries," she shouted as she walked through the door. "Come see, look, look at them, the beads are now linked with gold." She related to everyone there about the day of her mother's parting from grandmother Gaetana, and the touching story of how on the wharf in San Giovanni her grandmother had wound these very beads around her mother Bella's hands and told her daughter of their spiritual linking. The Lord rewarded their devotion to His Life and to His Mother with gold links, not extracted from the pits of the deep hard rock gold mines of this earth, but from His celestial vault of graces and His Holy Spirit of Love.

In spite of her age and crippled legs, Chiara made it her mission to visit all of her friends and family—and there were many—to witness and share her miracle. The golden links continued to strengthen the spiritual bond connecting Chiara to her mother in a new and wonder filled way.

CHAPTER 19

THE BUTTER BOX

The butter box was too large for its intended purpose. It was made over seventy years before Rico had come along and brought Lars' farm. The Scandinavian carpenter-turned-farmer who had designed it had held his greed on a tight leash, but now it was barking uncontrollably, and as his eager hands let go, it turned on its master and took a deep bite. Lars sense of reality became convoluted, and as evidenced by the size of the box, took up temporary residence in his imagination. Obsessed with the thought that his box had to be much larger than all of his neighbor's butter boxes, he allowed himself to get carried away.

It was a time when butter boxes were in use. After the cream was churned into butter and the buttermilk separated with a butter paddle, it was finally pressed into forms. The customary boxes could hold about a pound of butter.

When Lars Petersen had completed his carpentry, he stood back with hands on hips, viewed his handiwork, and couldn't believe what it had spawned. His conscience was assaulted when he realized the foolishness of his odyssey and particularly of his desire to make his neighbors envious. He had perverted its purpose, and became so distressed that he repented. In order to assuage his guilt and atone for this perversion, he employed his primitive skills and painted a biblical scene on its lid. But alas, no one in his family could find a use for the huge monstrosity, so he reluctantly stored it in the back of his work-shop where it remained there, forsaken, for many years.

Finally, it was handed down to the next generation, and since it still could not be utilized for its original intent, it became the recipient of old blankets, bonnets, and crinoline skirts, all crammed in to overflowing. To relieve the boredom of more than one rainy day, the young ladies of the house emptied and discarded its contents. With unbridled expectations, they used it as a chest to store their hopes and linens while waiting for their knights in shining amour to come galloping by and steal them away. Sadly, there were very few suitors, for they not only did not possess the qualities of typical Nordic beauties, but with the passing of time, tell tale signs of aging were taking their toll on the female occupants of the farmhouse.

Years passed but nowhere could be found the long awaited knights on their horses galloping up to the now sagging porch. And so, along with their hopes, in spiteful resignation, they delegated the now antiqued heirloom chest to the attic to live out its days, as was their lot, in abject loneliness.

Because of its heft, it took two of Lars's farm hands to lug it up the narrow steps to its exile.

With the passage of time, the primitively painted scene on the lid of the antique box had become barely visible. Beneath the peeling patches of old paint, Moses was depicted holding the tablets of God's Ten Commandments. On closer examination, what could still be seen if you brushed aside the flecks of green paint curling over the lid was the Roman numeral ten. Also on the tablets and a little above—it would have taken a magnifying glass and a squinting eye to make it out—there was the faint outline of the figure eight on the tablet. The paint continued to fleck and its holy command became obscured under the dust; years flew by, but not without evidencing the arrival of the new tenants in the attic. Occupying the rafters they roosted, happily producing more than a few generations of little winged ones.

The butter box remained in its lofty setting until the Norwegian farmer's house was sold to Rico.

CHAPTER 20

NEW ENGLAND FARMHOUSE

It was over one hundred years old; a relic of a farm. Lars had outlived his whole family and was no longer able to keep it up. He, too, was a relic, both farmer and farm having seen their day. It had been on the market for three years before Rico came by and saw it ripe for the picking. He offered Lars a pitiful sum, which at first he refused, where-upon Rico used all of his well-honed powers of persuasion. He quickly took full advantage of the old Scandinavian. "This place is a steal," he avariciously observed. The small sum he paid the old farmer would run out before the old man's heart did, leaving him to the inevitable fate of porch rocking and blank staring at the state home.

Rico did it again! Just last month he had trekked down to Long Island and manipulated poor old aunt Chiara out of her life's savings. He had conned her into signing over all of her stocks and bonds to him, and when they read her will, his cousins Gina, Sophia, and Carlo would be shocked but could do nothing. Now all he had to do was to get Chiara to come up here to Maine and persuade her to sign a new will, leaving the house and gallery to him.

Collecting his morning eggs from the nest in the coop behind the barn, he conceived a perfect plan. As he bent over to scoop them up in his grasping hands, he talked to the indignant hen. "My latest con on Long Island will pay off big. I, too, have a nest to feather."

A cracked cup hung on a nail in front of a rotting fly swatter on the barn door. The swatter hung motionless, a position it would have preferred in earlier days. Farmer Lars had used it in the milking barn as a weapon of mass destruction, aiding the cows when their tails were too slow in their swishing. Crooking the handle of the broken cup around his boney finger, he headed for the berry patch out back. Brushing aside the brambles, he squatted and picked the black berries, filling the cup. When he was done, he cackled to the rooster clawing at the low vines, "My cup will runnith over when the check from Auntie's mutual funds arrives, and what belonged to her and my cousins will be all mine."

Dragging a three-legged stool across the uneven linoleum kitchen flooring, Rico slid into the icebox door, bumping his head on its metal handle. At length he opened it-the selection was meager. He finally reached in and grabbed a slab of bacon from its fatty rash. After lighting the old coal stove, he slapped the pork into the black skillet and when it was sizzling, cracked an egg on top. It swam in the smoking grease until the bacon edges curled. With a flick of his finger, he brushed away the flying insects furiously buzzing around his meal and plugged in his latest purchase from the local thrift store. It was an antique of a toaster, whose bottom plate was still crusted with blackened crumbs from its previous owner, and its cord badly frayed and in need of repair.

Rico popped in his last two slices of stale bread and upturned the cup of berries onto the soiled oil-cloth covering the rotting wooden table. He slipped his finger into the handle of the cracked cup and poured himself a cup of reheated coffee. "A meal fit for a king," he said.

As usual, he dined alone, but no sooner had he lamented his fate than his little chicken wandered into the kitchen. The hen's head bobbed up and down and in frustration it pecked away at the bare linoleum floor. Not a crumb fell from the catch plate of the old toaster to reward its futile efforts, but the feathered jester amused Rico, and as he observed its pecking, he fell off the stool in a fit of laughter at his own poor attempt at humor. Regaining his sullen tone, he professed to the chicken, "There was a short time in my life when I was just like you. I pecked away and got nothing for my efforts until I figured out an easier way to fill my stomach." He picked up his fork and nourished himself with what he had taken from the little mother hen. Rico savored his egg all the more when he thought of how he had deprived the hen of her would-be chick. He envied her roosting, caring for her baby chicks and giving them protection under her wing. The more he thought of his own mother, the more depressed he became.

He entered into his usual state of brooding, and working up an intense dislike for the chicken, he suspiciously eyed the fowl and imagined her as a tasty bowl of soup.

CHAPTER 21

CRITTERS

When Rico had moved into the one-hundred-year-old farmhouse, the last place he had explored was the attic. When he did, to his horror he encountered a swarming hoard of bats, caught by surprise, for Rico's arrival was uninvited. With great animation, the critters had flapped around, indignant at his unpardonable intrusion. With their highly sophisticated sense of hearing, the sounds and echoes that determined Rico's very large size challenged them to dart straight at him while they screeched in harrowing pursuit. Rico had barely escaped their shrill cries and had determined that someday he would have to evict the tenants, and when that day came, he would have no mercy. Because they had roosted in their habitat for generations, they wouldn't be all that easy to get rid of.

The haunting remembrance of the ricocheting little critters bouncing off the rafters of the low ceiling had done damage to Rico's psyche. Because of the fright of that first spine-chilling encounter, he hadn't ventured up to the loft again. He kept his distance until one day he gave serious thought to a certain advantage to be gained. While in flight from the furious bats, his eyes caught a quick glance of an old wooden box in a corner, burdening the floorboards.

In the home stretch and coming too far with his Machiavellian plan to stop now, he decided to overcome that first terrifying experience with his third floor tenants.

Neighbor Abner had a hunting license. It was easier than Rico had imagined when he bribed him with free access to his back forty in return for a little favor.

With expert marksmanship, the unwanted occupants were quickly disposed of; upholding the law for endangered species was not even a consideration to these two country gentlemen. After Abner's job was completed with chilling accuracy, he descended the stairs with his smoking gun in hand and a bulging black bag slung over his broad shoulder, to go off in pursuit of much larger game on the back forty.

Rico reluctantly climbed the attic stairs. Ducking his head at the entrance he looked for tell tail signs that could have been overlooked and covering his head with his arm, he peered into every nook and cranny.

Satisfied that Abner had cleaned up all that his cocked finger had dispatched, Rico thought, "At last, the perfect hiding place for my ill-gotten stash," and he gleefully eyed the old wooden box.

CHAPTER 22

THE CHECK IS IN THE MAIL

At the very end of Rico's driveway, the first rays of sun began its castings as they lit up the mailbox, its tin skin displaying an array of honeybees and pinecones, a familiar sight on most mailboxes in Maine. Every morning Rico would trek down the driveway to see if his check had arrived. The check was the result of the biggest con he had ever attempted. He was all thumbs as he opened the half moon door, and with a tug, the missal fell into his hands. Wild eyed about the contents within, his wet palms moistened the envelope clutched in his hands, and his thoughts went back to Aunt Chiara and that profitable trip to Long Island. He stared down at his big pay off. Getting her to sign over her mutual funds and stocks to him was a touch of genius; his manipulations had served him well. He stood there hopping from one foot to the other, unable to contain himself, with his ill-gotten goods, signed, sealed, and delivered.

As he tore open the envelope, he realized that he had to get a grip before he went to the bank. When he became overly excited, his voice rose, and now his speech came fast and furious. "It's still early in the morning and not too many townsfolk will be there yet. I will cash the check that I got from the cashed-in mutual funds, and even though it will take a long time, I will have the teller put it in small bills. That will make quite a pile."

Victory was his at last, but it still was not enough. "Now I have to figure out a way to get my hands on the old homestead and gallery," and he walked towards town as he continued to weave his tangled web.

CHAPTER 23

USED AND ABUSED

When Rico got back to the farm, it was past noon. He rushed up to the attic and with great flourish he stuffed his stacks of bills into the oversized butter box. Rico chuckled. He would have enough spending money to last him for the rest of his days.

CHAPTER 24

KIDNAPPED

Chiara was now ninety-two years old. It was a Sunday morning, and Rico knew Cora and Nita would be at Mass. He waited patiently in his car, parked across the street from the estate, until he could see them leave. He was sure he could get the job done within the hour. He rang the chimed bell, and its noisy sound announced his unexpected arrival. Cora had left Chiara sitting in a nook in the foyer, her favorite Sunday napping place, the light shafting through the Tiffany windows. Her cat Bambi napped too, a fury question mark curled up on her lap. Rudely awakened, she wheeled herself to the door, and her chair almost tipped her over as she stretched out her hand to unlock it. When she saw Rico standing there looking wild-eyed and stranger than usual, she became frightened. His last visit was a disaster. Her fast-talking nephew had been to visit recently and had hoodwinked her into signing over most of the holdings in her portfolio. "Why did I let him do that?" she mused. Her usual pragmatism was eluding her these days. "Well, its too late now, but after he left I regretted my own rash behavior and I did repent of my foolishness. I must be cautious of Rico's flattering ways in the future."

His sweet sounding words and cajoling ways weren't working this time. When he said he came only for a very short visit, she intuitively suspected the worst, for Maine was a great many miles away. The clock was ticking and Rico had to work fast. He grabbed her spaghetti-thin wrist and twisted, urging her to come with him. Her arm began to hurt and when she refused to go, he became impatient and resorted to more force. Still recuperating from a serious bout with the flu, she was no match for Rico, who was strong and half her age. He ignored her pleadings when she told him that there was little chance of her surviving the ten-hour trip. All of her attempts to pull away were futile, and her whimpering doubled in intensity.

As Rico was packing a few of her belongings, she managed to reach the phone and frantically dialed Newell, who took some time to pick up, as he too, was getting on in age and was slow of step. Her gut feeling was confirmed when she realized that these would turn out to be the last words she would say to her lifelong friend. Her voice choked up as she whispered into the phone, "I have always loved you, Newell."

By the time Newell arrived at the front of her house, things had worsened. Rico was pushing Chiara into his car and she was crying hysterically all the while. Newell was traumatized by the scene he had witnessed. No one else was in sight. The neighbors, each of whom was acres away, were in their soundproof stucco-walled houses reading their Sunday papers or at church and were unaware of the drama unfolding outside their doors. All Newell could manage was to stand on the sidewalk and bite his nails while Chiara was being kidnapped right under his nose. He, too, was no match for the younger, stronger man.

As Rico sped off with his hostage, Newell fainted and hit his head on the curb and being short of stature he didn't have far to fall. As he fell a shard from his broken glasses imbedded in his jugular vein and he would have bled to death if Cora and Nita had not returned home to see him lying there in a pool of his own blood. They immediately rushed him to the hospital.

Less than a week would pass before Newell would receive the sad news that his dearest friend had died.

After a harrowing ten-hour drive, kidnapper and captive arrived at Rico's farmhouse in Maine. By then, Chiara was dehydrated. Without medical attention, her condition worsened. It was time for Rico to call an ambulance to whisk Chiara off to the community hospital where, immediately upon her arrival, he contacted a lawyer. It was Rico's intention to have his aunt make out a death bed will leaving the Guardi home and gallery to him. He called the lawyer, who by some strange coincidence, happened to be in nearby Portland vacationing.

Rico had been euphoric the week before when Scott suddenly appeared at his farmhouse to pay a visit. This unholy coincidence was perfect timing for his evil plan. Scott was from Sands Point on Long Island and his mother Lynn was Chiara's assistant at the Gallery. "Better to have a lawyer from a distance away than one of the locals prying into my business," Rico unwisely thought.

CHAPTER 25

ASH MAIL

Cousin Rico called Sophia and announced, "I've just had Auntie cremated." Sophia was stunned. Regaining her composure, she managed to gasp, "Who told you to do that?"

He replied, "I thought it would be nice to have Auntie's ashes scattered to the wind." Sophia thought of Chiara being so far from the home and away from all of the people she loved when she was forced to leave, and how she had died alone in a sterile, unadorned hospital room. She shuddered when she thought about how it had been rumored that Rico had taken Auntie from her home against her will. Knowing she had no proof and that no one would step forward to attest to this, she concentrated on the business at hand.

"What had made you even think of cremating our Aunt?" Sophia said, and with that, she gave him an ultimatum: "Either you comply with my wishes by sending the ashes home for a Christian burial, or I will investigate further, and if the rumors can be proven true, I will hire a lawyer and have the whole travesty investigated."

Reluctant at being exposed for the thief that he was, Rico was not about to call Sophia's bluff.

"Where are her ashes now?" Sophia demanded.

"I have them," he said. "I could send half of them in the mail if you insist, but I want to keep half a cup." Rico was enjoying the cat and mouse game.

Incredulous at his attitude, Sophia persisted. "Oh no! You won't do that Rico; all of her ashes must be buried in consecrated ground. Come down for the memorial Mass and bring all of the ashes with you. And furthermore, they could get lost in the mail. I don't imagine that Auntie would appreciate spending her eternity pigeonholed in a dead letter box at the post office."

Chiara had been a world traveler, and Sophia was horrified at the thought that her last journey, would be of her being sealed in a bubble envelope as her final resting place. Now her Italian genes were kicking in. "She is not a puff of smoke from your infernal cigars to be blown away and scattered in the wind," she yelled into the phone like a blast from a bugle. "Since the damage has been done, dear cousin, the only decent thing to do now is to bury her ashes with her sisters, as she so often requested, where she could finally rest in peace." Since Rico had not gotten permission from his cousins for the cremation, he knew, all too well, what his culpability involved. To legalize his hasty decisions after the fact, he frantically sent his cousins permission forms, using overnight mail to hasten their signatures. Then he anxiously called them, urging their signatures. Reluctantly, they agreed to his wishes for the time being. Having the signed papers in his hands, Rico balked again about coming down to Long Island. Sophia told him that if he didn't come with the ashes for the Mass, Father Giacomo was more than willing to drive up to Maine and personally pick them up. Fearing any contact with the crematorium, he agreed. Now they had assurance that Chiara's ashes would be coming home but they were saddened by the fact that there was no physical body to un-shroud this mystery.

CHAPTER 26

MASS OF CHRISTIAN BURIAL

Father Giacomo came to Sands Point to say the Mass of Christian burial at St. Peter's for Chiara, just as he had promised her he would when she attended his Ordination to the Priesthood. Belligerently, Rico made the trip from Maine for the services and brought with him the urn with what he said were Chiara's ashes. Until the last minute, he still belligerently wanted to "scatter them in the wind," but, outnumbered by his cousins and caught in the crosshairs, he finally conceded. He had to have her ashes buried or they would be "digging up the dirt" of his unhallowed ground.

Chiara's urn with her cremains occupied a place by the window in the back seat of Father Giacomo's rented black car. This unusual seating would have normally been in the rear of a hearse, but Father Giacomo and his mother Sophia wanted to honor her memory when they passed, in silent testimony, the hallmarks of her astonishing life.

They made their way through the busy morning traffic of downtown Sands Point where the seedlings planted so many years before were now tall and magnificent trees, giving time honored weight to their purpose, graciously bowing their branches to form a semi-arch of shelter where motorists passing through could momentarily abandon themselves to their verdant primordial embrace.

Still called the Main Street of Sands Point, it was now a broadened boulevard and Giacomo and his mother rode as slowly as the traffic allowed, first passing Chiara's beloved Guardia Gallery which impressively towered over all of the other buildings on the avenue. As they continued on, they marveled at the magnificent sight of the prestigious North Shore Library. It had been built up and around the original McGuffey one-room schoolhouse, where as a child Chiara had played at being a librarian. She went on to serve her community as head librarian on these very premises for many years.

Giacomo slowed down to an even slower pace when they passed the beautiful little gem in the crown: "the sleeping place," where in a very short time, Chiara's lifelong search would be realized. Just past the churchyard and within walking distance of the wide boulevard, stood the magnificent home Michael had built for his family. Its singular mounting beckoned all to come inside and see the powerful kitchen ceiling fresco, depicting Michael and Bella's love—their lives of sacrifice and service, which created and inspired such a beautiful American family.

When they reached the end of the boulevard, still standing by the dock, but in disrepair, they came to Fiona's boarding house, now under the ownership of her daughters, where Papa's vision of giving his family a new and better life had been conceived.

The tribute to Aunt Chiara's life had taken more time than the priest and his mother had expected. They had to make their way cautiously, for the traffic was heavy as Father Giacomo steered his car in the direction of the church for the funeral Mass of Christian burial. Making up for lost time, he hurried up the steps of the church, his cassock billowing behind him as he held tight to the vessel clutched in his hand. This would be Chiara's last visit to her beloved church. With great sadness, Giacomo entered the sacristy to vest and prepare his eulogy.

Gina, Sophia, and Carlo knelt in the front pew. They remembered when they were young children kneeling with Chiara in their midst on those sunny Sunday vacation mornings. Only now they were flanked by black funereal bouquets and the kneelers were still unpadded, but mercifully, time had added cushioning to their once bony knees.

They were astonished when they were suddenly assaulted by an onslaught of people coming at them from all directions. At first, they thought they were family and friends rushing up to give condolences, customarily offered in the vestibule after a funeral service. What ensued in the next half hour was stunning. These unheard of interruptions seemed to be whizzing by in fast motion, and the urgency with which they presented themselves was shocking. Descending upon them, one after another, were Chiara's trusted friends and family, each one demanding their attention.

With daughter Jenny's arm protectively around her mother's shoulder, the first accuser to approach was Cousin Joanne. She excitedly told her cousins not to trust cousin Rico. It seemed that she had had many uncomfortable encounters with him and was very offended by the way he had treated Zia Chiara on his infrequent visits from Maine. She had heard rumors of, but had not actually seen, Chiara's kidnapping. With great animation, she said she was certain Chiara would not have gone away with Rico of her own volition. Her daughter, Jenny, a nurse, had looked in on her frequently and knew that the flu had taken its toll and that Chiara had known that her days were numbered.

Armed only with her own intuition and with no legal proof to back it up, Joanne loudly expressed her frustration. She warned her cousins to be careful in any future dealings with Rico. She became so overwrought that her daughter had little success in quieting her mother and gently escorted her to the vestibule of the church.

The next outburst was from a woman whom they had never met before. She was one of Chiara's business associates at the Gallery. She introduced herself as Lynn, and as it turned out, she was lawyer Scott's mother—the same lawyer Rico had employed to make out a new will for Chiara to sign on her deathbed in that small hospital room in Maine.

"Please believe me. My son Scott did not know that there was a will already in existence," said Lynn. As her voice rose nervously, it cracked, and she became more agitated as she tearfully stated that her son was a "good boy, you have to believe me. If he had known that there was another will, with other inheritors, he never would have attempted going through with that imposed death-bed will."

The mother begging mercy for her son under the shadow of the beautiful statue of the Madonna looking down from the side altar brought a sense of consolation and dignity to her ramblings. Now visibly shaken, she continued, stating, "He never broke the law in his whole life. Please believe me, he didn't know. I beg you, please don't pursue this. His reputation is at stake. My boy is a good person."

The Grand Swindle was, it turned out, a devious plot perpetrated by Rico's planning alone. Unbeknownst to Scott, there was another will and other heirs out there.

The morning after Chiara had been admitted to the community hospital, Rico and Scott had stood at the door of her room, legal papers in hand, ready for the first signing. They were surprised when they peered through the window in the door to see her little bare cot empty and being prepared for the next terminal patient. Before they could procure Chiara's death-bed signature on a new will, the first morning light had shafted its glorious Maine rays through the small hospital room window. Absorbing the radiance of its heavenly transport, Chiara's soul was carried up into the world of her long—awaited belonging, but not before her final act of justice had prevailed. Chiara always did have a noble-spirited sense of fairness.

The pews were rapidly filling up. Chiara was the pillar of North Shore society, and for many years had contributed to its cultural richness. Seated in the row behind the grieving nieces and nephew was her dear friend, Newell. He quietly slipped across the pew to get closer, and with a tap on her shoulder, he got Sophia's attention.

Choking back his tears, he announced in a shaky but strong voice for the whole congregation to hear, "Chiara was murdered. It was Rico who was responsible. He forced her to go all the way to Maine when she was very weak from the flu. Chiara called me that dreadful day. I rushed over, but it was too late. When I got there, Rico was forcing her into his car. She was yelling that she didn't want to go with him. I couldn't help her when she needed me most."

Rico, seated nearby, heard every word Newell said. His head was down, but he was not in prayer. He was smiling. "Oh yes," he mused, "I wonder if I can have a chat with Newell later. When I get my hands on all that money, I know he'll be hard to approach but I might just give it a try." At that moment, Sophia turned and saw the expression on Rico's face. Why did she feel like she was sitting in a shark's cage?

Only half an hour had elapsed, but by the time Father Giacomo walked out on the altar, the three Guardis in the front pew felt battle weary from the war of words they had just endured. The rude display of unholy events, that had played out directly in front of the Altar of God, was left hanging in the air as the sleepy altar boy swung his incense bowl and its smoke intermingled with this strange web of intrigue.

The service began.

Father Giacomo's eulogy was inspired, giving well-deserved tributes to his great aunt. Great nephew Roberto sang the beautiful hymn, "Be Not Afraid." His voice and rendition reminded his mother Sophia, Aunt Gina, and Uncle Carlo of that other great singer so very long ago, on Sunday vacation mornings, whose voice also rose to the rafters and blessed the congregation. Newell leaned forward again, but this time he was calmed by Roberto's spiritual rendition and, caught up with emotion, he whispered to Gina, "How could Roberto know that his selection was your Aunt's favorite?"

After services when the bereaved lingered in the vestibule to console one another, Newell approached Maria, Sophia's daughter, and asked her if she had heard and understood what he had said in the church.

To make sure she was fully informed, he pulled her aside in the foyer and retold her of the frightening day of the kidnapping. Showing his frustration, his forehead broke out in beads of sweat as he confessed his weakness at the time she had needed him the most, recounting how he had fainted on the sidewalk and was rendered helpless after Rico forced Chiara into his car. As there were no other witnesses to this travesty, his word had been doubted. After all, the neighbors said, "Newell was elderly and the supposed kidnapper was her own nephew. We didn't see a thing." And in fact they hadn't. Most of the family and neighbors could not imagine, even Rico, doing such a shocking thing. No one took Newell seriously and brushed off his version as an old man's confusion. Maria too had heard these rumors before, but now she was giving more credence to Newell's account. She had known him for many years as Chiara's trusted friend and knew him to be an honorable man.

CHAPTER 27

HORNSWOGGELING

Rico informed his cousins that the will could not be found, but he was quite aware that it was in a safe deposit box at Chiara's bank in Sands Point. Carlo suspected as much, and with a few carefully worded persuasive phone calls to Rico, the will was produced. Rico then demanded that he and his own lawyer be co-executors, thus being able to continue to manipulate all of the legal proceedings. Unacceptable legally and morally, they refused. Already warned at the Funeral Mass of Rico's exploitation of her son by Chiara's friend Lynn, cousin Joanne's reservations and Newel's startling witness, the rightful heirs became justifiably suspicious. They insisted on Sophia being co-executor of the found will. Within her legal rights, she successfully retained her own lawyer.

The bulk of Auntie's holdings, which Rico had conned her into signing over to him just months before, would be contested, and the will would take years to probate and would be dragged through the courts. He caved and agreed to probate the will. "Even so, I still have time to figure out how to get my hands on the old family homestead and Guardi Gallery," he murmured under his breath.

CHAPTER 28

WHAT GOES AROUND

Out of all of the states in the union, it is Maine that God had chosen to be the first in the country to be greeted with His first morning rays. The inhabitants accepted His blessing gratefully as a harbinger of a bright new day, but this was not going to be so for Rico.

"Why can't anyone take care of me? Do I even have to make my own meals?" Rico asked as he entered the kitchen and pulled hard on the frayed wire hanging from the ceiling. The attached dim light bulb had an eerie glow that cast its shadow on the worn linoleum counter and played tricks on his eyes. "Toast and butter will have to do," he complained. As he enjoyed his own distracted murmurings, he jammed a thick piece of sliced bread into the toaster. As usual, the relic sputtered and slivered sparks shot out of the wall socket.

After his meager repast, he went up to bed unaware of the events unfolding below him.

Rico's life was about to come full circle, but not of the unifying kind as in the memorial marker at Chiara's sleeping place.

The antique toaster had provided its last meager meal. At first, there was a distant crackling hum, the sound of interlocking wires burning and sparking within the wall connection. There would be no evidence of the culprit crumbs on its plate as the sparks fell like red-hot coals upon straw-strewn floorboards and headed for the dry wooden stairs. The embers snaked around the banisters and rocketed up and they quickly became a wall of fire on the top landing. Roaring down the hallway they diabolically headed, as if prearranged, directly for Rico's room. Billowing smoke seeped under his door and swirled angrily around his bed. He awakened with burning eyes and nostrils, which slowed his progress as he clawed his way out of the room. The hallway was a firestorm. In panic, he crawled on his belly and made his way to the stairs where, without a thought to his burning body, flung himself headlong to the landing below.

Not knowing how he got there, he found himself outside in the cold night air. Within seconds of jumping off the porch, the entire farmhouse turned into a blazing inferno. He staggered in shock, not feeling the driveway gravel cutting into his scorched feet. Was all of this another one of his recurrent dreams? "Am I on the highway again, running away from the orphanage?" he wondered.

When he reached the bottom of the driveway, he found himself clutching onto the only standing structure—the mailbox. The charmingly painted yellow and black honeybees on its surface, where they previously endured the unfortunate residency of being forced to witness the fruits of Rico's stealth, seemingly transformed themselves into a hoard of swarming angry bees. Rico's pain was now so severe that he imagined he could feel them as they flew off the box and covered him with their poisonous venom. This stinging, surreal disaster played out before him as his farmhouse burned to the ground.

The brilliant morning rays were not a blessed harbinger for Rico. They only revealed more clearly the charred remains of what had been. His awakening to what had happened was brutal. There was nowhere to turn and he felt imprisoned within his fractured soul. Rico's god of greed could not help him now. The box in the attic consumed his thoughts, as he swayed before a pile of ashes, which only a short time ago had been the converted hope chest filled with the results of his avarice.

Trying to salvage anything was futile. Sifting through the ashes left nothing but a strange little mass at Rico's feet. The barest semblance of green flecks, curled around tiny particles of cinders suddenly emerged from the mound.

As if in an instant, a strong Maine wind carried these sinister atoms up into the sky. They flew far into the atmosphere where they morphed into a small, strange cloud. Higher and higher, the cloud rose until it could no longer be seen by anyone on earth.

Chiara and her little sisters frolicked on the golden shore. Angelic orbs of light bounced in and out of their pirouettes, and with childlike abandon, the sisters played in the silver mist, twirling and dancing across the sea of glass before The Throne.

So enraptured were they with their celestial union, they hardly noticed at all when the small cloud disintegrated in the atmosphere below and the ashes of greed "scattered in the wind."

PART II

RISING FROM THE ASHES

CHAPTER 29

RUN RICO RUN

When Rico's farmhouse burned to the ground, his whole world went up in smoke and with it, all the money he had hidden in the butter box. Because he had spent the day squatting too close to the smoldering embers, sifting through the ashes of his wretched life, he was oblivious to the blisters beginning to form on his body; clusters of tiny balloons taut and ready to pop. Soot clung to his clothing, and black dust overshadowed his soul, consuming it in the darkness of despair. With his last vestige of pride, Rico pushed himself up on his haunches and stood upright to assure himself that he was still a man. Rising from the ashes, he knew he was doing the Guardi family proud. They were all blessed with the gift of survival, and Rico had more than his share.

Running away from his Maine neighbors, he headed for the highway, leaving behind his strange behavior and the fiery furnace of a farmhouse to be weighed in the balance. His progress was labored as in a dream, but he pressed on with his burned legs and stiff, robotic strides as he attempted to separate himself from his disreputable past. Unwanted images of his recurring nightmare of another harrowing escape generated unwelcomed flashbacks of the time he had broken loose from his six years of confinement at the orphanage. Twenty years had passed since he had slid down the slippery slide, bilking and bamboozling anyone who crossed his path. Laying in the wake was the appalling humiliation of his unsuspecting victims, and worse still, his systematic destruction of many innocent lives. You could almost smell the flint as synaptic signals in Rico's brain sparked these disturbing memories. He sensed the merciless axe of retribution being laid to the root, and he knew that his day of reckoning was at hand.

CHAPTER 30

THE PEACH STONE

A day had passed, and Rico found himself in the center of a small harbor town in Portland, Maine.

It was dawn again, and the first brilliant rays of sun forced the greengrocer to shade his eyes as he squinted and keyed the lock in the door of his shop and opened up for the day. His stomach churned from the acrid smell of overripe fruit as he disappeared into the darkness, only to return a few minutes later with a heavy crate of imported peaches hoisted on his shoulder. His back was turned, and as he filled an empty wooden bin attached to the storefront, he did not see Rico crouching behind the garbage dumpster. Waiting until the man reentered his shop, and with fingers still blackened from ash sifting, he reached down and snatched a golden peach from the newly stocked bin. The fruit immediately betrayed the significance of its smell as its pungent odor triggered an intoxicating effect on his reasoning. It would prove to be the catalyst for his astonishing transformation and somehow, he knew that he would never steal again.

He needed time to think things out. "Where do I go from here?" he said as he reluctantly returned to his unappetizing habitat. As he squatted down to ponder his fate, he spied a soiled McDonald's box harboring a half-eaten burger in the trash that spilled out of the dumpster. Flicking off the limp pickles, Rico swallowed it in one gulp, flies and all, as he pondered his fate.

His thoughts went back to that pivotal morning when his father had abandoned him at the orphanage and they had had the only meaningful conversation he could remember. Giovanni had told him of his desire to return to the old country when his time had come. He wanted his remains to be laid to rest with his ancestors at their sleeping place beneath the peach trees in their orchard in San Giovanni. Rico had been eager to please his father, so he agreed. If he had known what was awaiting him behind the orphanage door he would not have been so hasty in his decision. But as often happens, fate intervened and Gio's wayward life in his adopted country had weighed heavily on his soul. In his final days, he had repented of his sins, especially those he had committed against his parents, and received the forgiveness of Divine Mercy. In further atonement, he had abandoned his own desires and was interred with his parents in the family plot at Heaven's Gate Cemetery on Long Island.

Rico continued on his journey, not knowing where he was headed or why. He thought about everything he had spent his whole, amoral life trying to accomplish. In between small bites of his peach, for he was obsessed with it lasting as long as his journey, he shouted to the wind, "I can stay in this country no longer. My cousins are all on to me, and the law is closing in. I have to make my way to San Giovanni and find out what had possessed my father to want to return there."

The salt in the sea air cleared his head and his canines furiously gnawed at the stringy threads on the last bit of flesh stubbornly clinging to the peach stone. Rico savored the final shreds of the stolen fruit, and when there was nothing left but a hard wooden shell, its jagged edge caught on his tongue; bleeding and scratched, it headed straight for his throat. Before its fatal slide, he managed to cough it up and with it, his barren life of frustration was unleashed. A sudden rage consumed him and as he regurgitated, the pit flew out and fell onto the moist sand at his feet. Raising his heel, he stomped it into the sandy loam as his final act of defiance. Americo, the master con artist, conned himself into believing he was finally rid of the country whose name he bore, but the grains of sand had already started their own downward spiral into the hour glass of time to tell a different story.

The State of Maine is not known for its cultivation of peach trees, so it was a strange thing that this unintentional planting would become the harbinger of things to come in Rico's life. The pit would grow into a tree beside the waters and would yield its fruit in due season, but not exactly like the fruit from which it came.

CHAPTER 31

IF YOUR SINS ARE LIKE SCARLET

Another day passed. Turning off the highway, Rico suddenly found himself facing the vast expanse of the Atlantic Ocean. The roar of the waves crashed against the shore. The cadence of its rhythm pounded in his eardrums, and it echoed, "Which way will you take, Rico, which way will you take?" Teetering on the precipice of indecision, his thoughts collided and became a cylindrical compression of good and evil, which ignited in his soul and waged a war of moral choices. He knew that his decision would change the course his life forever.

Strong sprays blew in from the sea with cruel affliction, and its vortex picked up sharp crystals and mixed them with the salty mist, blanketing Rico's body, and cutting into his wounds still raw and bleeding from the journey. He hadn't the energy or will to move his toes, which were dug deep into the cold wet sand. He had reached the end of his endurance.

In desperation, he raised his arms to the heavens and prayed. As he did, he naively thought that he would have to yell in order to be heard above the screeching sea gulls. In a voice that pierced the heavens, he shouted. His plea was framed in the humility of a man who had suddenly come into a profound awareness of his own sinfulness.

"Please do not leave me stuck in this sand forever, Lord, move me on to embrace Your Way. My soul agonizes for all the pain I have caused others but most of all the pain I have caused You."

Forgiveness came swiftly for the repentant sinner, and as the incoming tide swept the shore, a more powerful anointing swept Rico's soul and he was slain in the Spirit of God. As he fell forward, unseen forces were at work. The Almighty baptism inundated him with its curative waters, and Rico's healing began. The sand was soft and pliant, and as his head hit the sand, it carved out a hollow pillow. The last thing he saw was a strange shape carved by the wind on a nearby dune. It was the specter of a young boy.

He fell into a deep sleep and dreamed of Joey, the only friend he had ever had, who, for the sake of justice in his unjust world, had died at the orphanage. Joey appeared before him as a beautiful angel surrounded by a blinding light. Floating above his hand was a radiant golden cross atop a jeweled sphere. The water in the orb was holy, and with it, Joey sprinkled his friend with the waters of salvation.

When Rico awakened, a gentle breeze encircled him. As he inhaled its sweetness, his thoughts became the repository of imaginary whisperings, which converged into a haunting wind song; its seductive refrain beckoning him to a place he had never known. "Return to the homeland of your ancestors Rico," it said.

A new and profound sense of self enveloped Rico, and he realized a complete harmony of his soul and body. He was experiencing a metanoia, a spiritual conversion; a transforming change.

"For the first time in my life, I feel like a whole person," he said. "I am a part of all that I can see."

Rico rejoiced exceedingly in his heart. He bowed his head in awe. As he did, he saw that his burned and blackened fingers were now as white as the small conch shells clinging to the wet strands of his matted hair, and all of the wounds that had covered his scarred body were gone. His spirit was reborn, and like a phoenix rising from the ashes, it soared heavenward, and was at one with its Creator. Americo Guardi knew that he belonged.

His eyelids stuck together with wet grains of sand and Rico had to squint in order to barely make out the behemoth lumbering towards him as he looked towards the horizon. One of the largest steamships in the world, the Victorian, was heading into port. "It will take me to where I am destined to go," he reflected. "I will get a job in its galley as a chef's helper, or maybe I can work in the meat carvery."

Rico left the land of his birth with a quiet dignity. Effortlessly, from a small quick-flowing rivulet, a lifetime of pent-up tears flowed down his face and into the pool swirling around his feet. They mingled with the outgoing tide and went out into the sea of forgetfulness, and his sins were remembered no more.

CHAPTER 32

CROSSING OVER

The first thing he did after he boarded ship was to seek out an "Apostle of the Sea," for he had a strong need to confess his sins. He found the cruise ship chaplain in a small, private cabin on mid deck. Father Daniel Drake was tall and slight in width and a mop of thick auburn hair framed his ruddy face. Rico could see the love coming from the chaplain's deep blue-green eyes, and was instantly put at ease and somehow knew that the Father would listen to him with his heart. He talked about his sinful past and all the suffering he had caused others and himself but most of all the pain he had caused his Maker. Then he told his confessor about the struggles he had gone through, running away from all that was unholy in his life, and finally, in desperation, he turned his life over to the Lord.

Father Drake was wont to talk in parables and was well known on board for being so easily understood. He spoke to Rico of bridges, saying that the only toll we had to pay was one of love and repentance. He said that, on our life's journey, the bridges connected us to God, and that we had the free choice to take the first step towards Him and continue crossing the bridges in His Way and in His Truth and in His Life; and that he would be waiting for us to join Him on the other side. Or we could choose to ignore Him.

Rico had many sins, and his confession took a very long time. After he was absolved, he knew that he was forgiven and determined that he would spend the rest of his life making amends to the people he had harmed. Priest and penitent prayed together; their daily visits continued throughout the journey, and their comradeship continued throughout their lives.

He surprised himself, for the old Rico would have stowed away and stolen his passage. But now, here, he wanted to pay his own way, embarking on his journey by seeking employment. Heading for the galley in the lower deck, he signed up for a one-way hitch. Two positions were still available; one was as a chef's helper and the other a meat carver's apprentice. He felt he was more suited to the latter because of his affinity for knives. In earlier days, his unrealized fantasy was to become a knife thrower in the circus.

In spite of the fact that the interviewer, the master carver, did not know a thing about Rico's background, which would qualify him as his apprentice, he was inexplicably drawn to him and hired him on the spot. The instructor, who was known to all on board as Eduardo the Meat Carver, was inquisitive about this engaging young man. Every morning at dawn, before he began training his eager pupil, they could be seen leaning on the rail on top deck absorbed in deep discussion.

They were sharing their lives. Eduardo unburdened his heartbreaking past to his new friend. He told him that his grandfather, Mario, had been a meat carver too, and that he had served a life sentence in prison for murder. Mario's son, Alberto, was unable to bear the shame of this disgrace in their village and finally succumbed to the little murders on the slanderous tongues of his neighbors and died of shame. Eduardo confided to his new friend that he could no longer endure his father's early demise and left the farm in the care of a migrant worker and his daughter, Anna, and signed on to the first ship that came into port, the Victorian. The only position available to him was that of a meat carver, a trade his grandfather had taught him, one that Mario knew all too well.

After a few short weeks under Eduardo's scrupulous tutorage, Rico qualified as his assistant. When off duty, they would amaze their shipmates by brandishing their knives in sync. They gave riveting performances of *katsuramuki*, a very difficult Japanese technique of carving. When some of the passengers heard of their extraordinary feats, they, too, excitedly crowded into the small galley to share in their mesmerizing exhibitions.

They preferred to do their carving in the galley and were not tempted to apply their skills on the gourmet tables on top deck, which catered to the idiosyncrasies of the well-to-do passengers. But there were glorious sunny days that lured them to top deck, when a change of venue was welcomed. Rico's premier performance with the elite found him stationed tableside, with his mentor, at an exclusive area at the far end of the deck. At first impression, he was fraught with fear when he encountered his meeting with a few privileged hoi aristoi who were extreme gourmands, approaching the food table with quick short steps, trotting eagerly like salivating piranha, awaiting their newest bizarre delicacy.

The Arabians prized their marinated camel backs and the Chinese excitedly relished deep fried snakes, grasshoppers, and scorpion. Being savored with unrestrained glee and tickling many an Asian fancy were *balut*, fetus duck eggs still festooned with their tiny feathers. There were Scandinavians who were known to work themselves up to a frenzy of praise when *lutefisk* was on the menu. The dried codfish was first soaked with lye, and if overcooked by the chef, it would turn into soap. Few partook of this delicacy, as it was foul and odiferous, and when eaten by the uninitiated, it was described as being similar to passing a kidney stone. But what made the diners pant with wild anticipation was *fugu*, the deadly Japanese blowfish which, if not prepared by the skill of a licensed chef, could paralyze or kill the eater. This epicurean's Russian roulette brought out the gambler in some of the more adventurous gastronomes who sporadically met their demise while eating it.

When he was subjected to a particularly deviant cuisine, Rico was at first repulsed. But as one can get used to hanging by his thumbs if he has to, Rico gradually became accustomed to the strange array of the odd repasts of the privileged. He fastidiously plated the peculiar concoctions, creating works of art on the Victorian's royal bone china.

Rico often was appalled by some of the gluttonous appetites of the gourmands as they ate their way across the Atlantic. Some of the more unusual victuals were particularly repellant to him, but none so much as when he found himself serving thinly sliced sharks fin. Eduardo had told him that the fin stabilized and balanced the fish and steered it to its destination, but when it was caught and the fin cut off, the poor mammal was thrown back into the water alive, where it fell to the bottom and died a slow death. Wasn't this what had happened to him that morning when he found himself abandoned by his parents, more embarrassed than frightened on the orphanage porch in the middle of nowhere? "I was rendered finless by my father, Gio. No wonder I was unbalanced," he thought. "Was this the reason for my lifetime of instability, making it almost impossible for me to navigate my way through life?" He thought about his fall from grace and the agony of his spirit's protracted demise.

Rico now understood who he was and who he was meant to be. In some way, he knew that he would be heard, and strange words fell from his lips.

"Oh God," he cried out, "I know I am undeserving, but would You graft a new fin on my back?"

It was not so strange a prayer for the One who listened.

The ocean voyage was coming to an end, and Rico had learned more from Eduardo than slicing and dicing. Their friendship had slowly evolved into a father-son relationship, and as they talked about Eduardo's grandfather Mario and Rico's great-grandfather Paulo, the patriarch, neither realized the obvious— that these two men had been so infamously connected.

The large oasis on the ocean soon found its way to Italy's spectacular Amalfi Coast on the southern coast of Italy, where, with its two extraordinary passengers, it was moored in safe harbor.

While at sea, Eduardo entrusted his farm to a young itinerant farmer. Every year he returned to San Giovanni to spend his summers working the farm, but now it was his feet he intended to plant in the rich soil of Naples. He had made many voyages back and forth on the Atlantic Ocean, but his days as master carver had come to an end.

From generation to generation, the tongues still wagged in the village, retelling the age-old scandal of his grandfather's violent deed. Eduardo prayed that this year would be different. Now he would have his fine young friend to distract the old ones from their pastime and ease the shame of his disgrace. As soon as the Victorian docked, he invited Rico to come and spend some time with him before pursuing his quest. Needing to meditate on his incredible spiritual awakening, Rico was happy to oblige. The tragedy involving their ancestors so many years before was about to have a very powerful effect on their lives.

CHAPTER 33

ANNA AND THE READERS

Alfonso, an ambitious migrant worker, was itching to settle down in one place. So when Eduardo needed someone to work his farm when he was at sea, Alfonso's industrious reputation preceded him, and he was hired on. The hard life of farming wasn't to his beautiful gypsy wife's liking, and after a year she ran off with an itinerant vintner. Their daughter was only six at the time, and soon little Anna was forced into chores far beyond her tender years. From dawn to dusk, she and her father labored, and in time, their husbandry skills became the envy of all of the other farmers in the valley. They even converted the barn into a few comfortable rooms which they rented out to tourists every summer.

Her life was busy and full on the farm, but Anna was not content. While tending sheep, she often wished she could join the neighborhood girls from the surrounding farms as they skipped down the dirt path behind the pasture. Every morning heading for the local state school, they recited their lessons in sing-song repetition. She longed to be with them but knew it was only a dream that could never be realized. That is, until a fortunate coincidence came her way and changed her life.

She was ten years old when Henry Evans, a British tourist, came to spend a summer in the barn and became so enchanted with the area that he purchased an abandoned farmhouse down the road. Henry was an English university professor who retained his flat in London where his library was equal to none. Its lofty shelves were stocked with a plethora of eclectic readings. He could often be seen browsing bookshops for first editions and prided himself when he found an 1836 first edition of Truman and Smith's McGuffey Readers, the best-known schoolbooks in American education in the nineteenth century. He proudly brought the Readers with him to his small farm in San Giovanni and at once hand carved a rustic wall shelf to display them. They remained there, decorative and unused, until he received a visit from his little next door neighbor.

She asked him what was so special about those books up there on the pretty shelf, to have such an honored place in his home. He reached for the smallest one of the set, the Primer, and placed it reverently in her hands. As she opened it, the corners of her eyes moistened. She handed it back to him, blushed, and shrugged her shoulders in a gesture of humiliation.

Henry was saddened when he realized that she could not read a word. Every day from that time on, Henry did what he did best. He taught Anna to read and write, and learn the English language using the extraordinarily rich store of knowledge from the McGuffey Readers.

Each summer, for the next six years, Anna completed another Reader, until finally she had mastered them all. With the most excellent of tutors and Anna's keen intellect, her mind and character were fortified, and she reached her full potential. Anna, as it turned out, was Henry's most gifted student.

CHAPTER 34

TRUE PERCEPTIONS

The aroma of sauce and sausage filled the air, as Eduardo and Rico walked through the door of the farmhouse. Early that morning, Anna had baked her bread, simmered her sauce, and filled the wooden bowl with peaches and grapes freshly picked from the arbors. Her favorite part of the preparations was in creating an antipasto. She would arrange black olives from the grove, mozzarella from her sheep's milk, and an assortment of green yellow and purple vegetables from her garden. These were to be served with small bowls of aioli. On the table, she placed one large bowl of olive oil, which would be passed around the table to dip her fresh baked bread into. It was Anna's gift to serve.

Now that Eduardo was home to stay, Anna and her father, Alfonso, would have to move out of the farmhouse and occupy the tourist barn, which they didn't mind at all.

From the moment that Rico, now thirty-six, first encountered Anna, he was smitten. The difference of twenty years was not at all uncommon in the rural, Italian countryside. He praised her cooking and delighted in her perfect pronunciation of the English language. It reminded him of his Aunt Chiara's, smooth and flawless. Hadn't they both been schooled in the McGuffey

Readers? Many times, he had sent up prayers for Aunt Chiara to forgive him of his most serious sin. Rico had a long way to go before forgiving himself.

In the evenings, Rico and Anna sat under the arbor and held hands, much like Grandma Bella and Grandpa Michael had on the riverbank underneath the bridge so many years before in their courting days. Rico told Anna about his life in America, and as he did, his own perceptions changed, and the rosy picture he painted became true to him and not at all the America from which he had escaped.

"I cannot put it off any longer. In the spirit of my father's final wish, I must visit the graves of my great grandparents," he said to Anna. "As it is only a day's journey, surely your father will have no objections if you come with me." She would have followed Rico anywhere, and she ran to her father to get his consent. As he trusted his daughter and knew he had raised her well, he gave his permission at once.

"I have come to your home, now you must come to mine," he said to Eduardo.

The triune journeyers traveled by donkey cart, lumbering along the dirt roads slowly enough for them to take pleasure in the beautiful Naples countryside. It had scarcely changed since Bella and Michael had traversed the same dirt roads almost a century before. Nearing their destination, they crossed the old wooden bridge where a highly favored and powerful love was born, strong enough to span time and space. Rico imagined that he had felt their sweet sprits brushing past him and the strumming of Michel's mandolin leading them on.

Memories of the stories of Grandma Bella's pet sheep, Baa, were sparked when they came upon a flock grazing on a grassy knoll. Rico wondered if they could have been originally sired by Baa, whose wool filled the quilt that still hung proudly in the entrance of the family gallery as a symbol of the family's sacrifice and service.

When they arrived near their destination, the panoramic view of the valley was as Rico had imagined. Alongside the broad dirt road leading to the farmhouse, they neared a peach orchard close to a small stream running through the meadow. It was late in season, and the heavy, ripe fruit lowered from their branches seeming to bow in reverence over a large, verdigris copper marker indicating the Sleeping Place of the saints interred below. The epitaph read, "Gaetana and Paulo Guardi Sleep Here, Together Forever."

As Eduardo and Anna watched, Rico fell to his knees on the sunbaked ground and as he prayed, he felt unworthy. "I do not deserve to be a member of this family to whom I have brought *dishonor*. Please tell me, Lord, how I can make amends for the horrible things I have done."

His answer was swift in coming when he thought that he had heard a drone of bees behind him. He ducked instinctively, afraid that he might be stung. But it was only the voices of a large group of people also intent on giving homage to their ancestors.

When he turned around, he was filled with fear when he recognized the cousins he had escaped from in America, and with them, his many aunts and uncles with all of their children. They had all come together in this little hamlet on the other side of the world for a very special family reunion at their ancestral home. One could lose count of all of the descendents of Gaetana and Paulo, for now there were many Guardi's.

They stared at each other as every jaw dropped. Not one was able to speak. It was a bittersweet reunion, for the joy that had brought them there, and the sudden realization of their need to forgive Rico for his past sins against them, had made them strange bedfellows.

Eduardo recognized the struggling of the family who were finding the situation difficult to deal with. He was an intruder in this unfolding drama. All at once, he was impacted by the realization that he had his part to play, when he noticed that he was the only one who saw a shaft of light piercing the verdigris memorial plaque at his feet.

He bent low and read the inscription on the marker. He was stunned when the obvious became apparent. There were many Paulos in all of the villages in the valley; it was a very common name. Having heard the name Paulo mentioned so many times with awe as the Saint of Forgiveness, he wondered why he had never made the connection that this was, in fact, the same Paulo who was his friend's great grandfather.

The marker, placed there so many years before, took center stage as Eduardo stood above it. He was in the orchard of the resting place of the man who was killed by his grandfather. He didn't have long to brood over his discovery, as something drew his attention. With a thud, an intrusive missile fell from a branch and hit him on the head. He yelled for all to hear, "What was that?" As if to emphasize its meaning, another took the same course. He picked up his fuzy assailants, knowing what he was supposed to do. With one cupped in each hand, he walked towards the outdoor kitchen, and the family, still stunned at the turn of events at their reunion, followed him.

Eduardo set out many wine glasses on the rough-hewn wooden tables. He filled them with wine, and after all were served; he put his skill to good use, sliced the peaches paper thin, and passed them around to the family. He told each of them dip their slice into their glasses of rich Taurasi wine.

Everyone's curiosity was aroused when Eduardo warned them that parts of a gigio worm were in their peach slices, and after dipping them, they must be discarded, for in doing so, tradition dictated, they would rid themselves of any hate eating away at their souls.

After they had discarded the slices and had drunk the wine, Eduardo continued.

"Paulo, your patriarch, had planted his peach trees in the rich soil of love, somehow knowing that one day his ancestors would gather together beneath their boughs. We must now make a circle, lock our arms together and forgive those who have injured us and those whom we have injured. In doing this we give tribute to the one who has taught us to imitate the example he gave with his final act. It was your sainted ancestor who so perfectly imitated our Lord's example when he followed Him in His ultimate act of forgiveness."

The Guardi family, including Eduardo and Anna, formed a circle and locked their arms together and all did as they were asked. It turned out to be a very glorious reunion.

One by one, each member of the family lined up for their blessing from Father Giacomo before the feast. The family had grown leaps and bounds, and all of the children and grandchildren of Bella and Michael reveled in preparing the magnificent celebration. Fredo's children, Carlo, Sophia, and Gina, were delighted to oversee all of the activities. Rico and Eduardo couldn't resist entertaining at the carving board, fascinating the audience with their awesome knife exhibition before they got down to the business of preparing the meal's entrée. Anna made her famous antipasto, and all of the elders scurried around cooking the sauce and pasta and setting the tables.

The old homestead buzzed with activity, while some of the children ran with the wind over the pasture in joyful abandon and others waded barefoot in the warm summer stream. The youngest petted the little lambs and carried them to Bella's meadow where they helped the children gather wild flowers to adorn the tables.

Rico knew that he and Anna would soon be married, and that he would take her back to America where they, too, would share their love of God by bringing service and sacrifice to all. Isn't that what the Guardi's were all about?

ACKNOWLEDGMENTS

The author wishes to thank her daughter, Mary, for her loving dedication and invaluable professional assistance in copyediting her story.

Her daughter Tina, for being the epitome of enthusiasm and belief in her mother's abilities, and for her wonderfully contagious enthusiasm.

A heartfelt thank you to son Daniel for his unwavering confidence in his mother's writing capabilities.

To son Robert, who thought his mother could do anything she put her mind to, even writing a book in her early eighties.

To her sister Jeanne, who patiently listened to her read this book aloud to her many times and remains her best friend forever.

To her brother, Felice, for his unconditional belief in his sister's untried capabilities.

To her daughters-in-law Janet and Paula for their loving support.

With deepest appreciation to her son, Father James, who inspired his mother to write this book, and his confidence that she could, and who indefatigably followed it up from its conception to its end.

Grateful acknowledgment to her publishing team at Westbow Press, particularly Dustin Gearlds, who made this challenging journey possible.

A very special thank you to Mary Higgins Clark for her invaluable advice and encouragement, which led the author into the unknown waters of the literary world until her story crossed over and found safe harbor.

CPSIA information can be obtained at www.ICGtesting.com
Printed in the USA
BVOW071627080212

282269BV00002B/2/P

9 781449 733797